IF I COULD LIVE AGAIN

a heart wrenching, thought provoking
novel that spans lifetimes

C. INGRID DERINGER

 FriesenPress

One Printers Way
Altona, MB,
R0G0B0
Canada

www.friesenpress.com

Claire Mulligan
Editor

Book Cover Design by Ingrid Deringer & Suzannah Hahrt

www.ingridderinger.com

ISBN
978-1-03-911959-8 (Hardcover)
978-1-03-911958-1 (Paperback)
978-1-03-911960-4 (eBook)

1. FICTION, CONTEMPORARY WOMEN

Distributed to the trade by The Ingram Book Company

Thanks

This story started as a short story and grew into a novel. It has been a labour of love from start to finish. Two people in particular made writing enjoyable.

My editor, Claire Mulligan, with her cheerful demeanour, encouraged me from day one.

My dearest friend, Suzannah Hahrt, who was always there to listen and lend a hand with her ideas and artistic talents and her enduring support. She also co-created the book cover with me.

Dedication

For my daughter Tania

"Know therefore, that from the greater silence I shall return... Forget not that I shall come back to you... A little while, a moment of rest upon the wind, and another woman shall bear me."

KAHLIL GIBRAN

The Beginning...

Writing a book is a tedious job, and many times I have thrown the pages aside and asked myself, "Why am I writing this?" Writing was never on my bucket list. Before I was compelled to write, I was living a comfortable life in a small hamlet called Bragg Creek in Alberta, just thirty minutes outside Calgary. I was an artist and an aspiring singer and loving my life. I had just gotten a scholarship to attend the Banff Centre and was on cloud nine. But then two things happened that changed the course of my life and made me take pen to paper: first my parents died, then I met Alex.

Going through my parents' belongings was heart wrenching, but it brought discoveries at every turn. You think you know someone until you go through their personal belongings. But one discovery had nothing to do with them. It had to do with me. In their closet on a top shelf were dozens of shoe boxes labeled "Sarah's Tales." These handwritten tales, or more precisely, transcripts of tales, had been written by my parents and were ones I had presumably told them when I was a small girl. Oddly, the tales stopped when I was around the age of six.

Now, my parents were very well-educated hippies who lived on a small hobby farm that my father inherited. They were bio-dynamic farmers, amateur artists and poets, pot-smoking partying, fairy dancing, drumming, homeschooling protesters for peace. You get the picture. I remember them alluding to my tales a few times when I was growing up, but it was usually only when they were high on mushrooms, blabbing on and on and laughing hysterically. But I never felt compelled to read them till I found them in their closet the week after their accidental deaths.

I sat down one afternoon and read every one of these tales. There were around a hundred of them. Although they were interesting, they didn't really mean much to me at the time, mostly because I remembered so little. They would have just been a footnote to my crazy, wild, wonderful childhood, and most likely would have stayed in my closet in the same shoe boxes till one day my own child would have discovered them and wondered what the heck they were. But all that changed when I met Alex, and then, damn it, there was no turning back. I needed to write this book. The one you are holding in your hands.

It is ultimately the story of Margaret. I have tried to be as accurate as possible by using Margaret's diaries and letters as well as information from people in her life who were still living at the time of writing. Margaret eventually stopped writing in her diaries, and there were fewer letters. At that point, I have told the story through the eyes of her family. I did have to use my imagination to fill in some of the gaps, but I feel I came very close to the truth of what happened.

I urge you to keep an open mind till the very end as I, myself, had to do. Let's begin . . .

BOOK ONE

Sarah, age four and a half

"*What are all those sticks in the sand, Sarah?*"

"*Those are my sisters, and these two little ones are my brothers.*"

"*Wow, you have a lot of sisters!*"

"*Yes, there are lots of them.*"

"*Where are you?*"

"*I'm right here, Mommy! I'm going to sing a song that I wrote to them because it is time for bed.*"

"*Well, that is nice that you sing to them.*"

"*Yeah, they like it, and I like it, too.*"

"*Where do you live?*"

"*On a farm with lots and lots of cows.*"

MARGARET
1925

The wind howled through the single pane windows. It was cold and dark outside. The sun wouldn't come up for hours.

"At least it isn't snowing," thought eight-year-old Margaret as she looked out the window across from the bed. Just then she heard her mother approaching.

"Get up, Margaret," her mother whispered loudly into her ear. "It's five in the morning already. We're going to the barn. I need you to stoke the fire and look after Annie. She be needin' changing, and she's screaming blue murder. Hurry up fore she wakes up the rest of them."

Margaret did not want to leave the warmth of the feather quilt and of her twin sisters on either side of her. She groaned as her feet hit the icy floorboards of the old farmhouse. She searched under the bed for her slippers, the ones with the double soles that Aunt Beatrice had knit for her. She heard the wind howling through the house; it was so cold. "Why didn't Ma stoke the fire before she left for the barn?" she wondered.

Margaret noticed that Annie's screams rose in pitch. Should she go to her or stoke the fire? She decided on the latter, and so by the time she got to her parent's room, Annie was purple with anger, and tears and snot covered her pretty freckled face.

She lifted her little sister up and stroked her back and rocked her before laying her down to change her diaper. She sang quietly as she changed her, wiped her face, and slipped a clean nightie over her head. She bundled her up in a flannel blanket and carried her to the kitchen. When she opened the oven door a rush of heat radiated out, and the two of them swayed and bounced as Margaret sang "Row Row Row Your Boat" till they both warmed up.

She was proud of herself that she was strong enough to hold Annie on her hip and get the porridge on the stove at the same time, just like her Ma would do. She was tall for her age and "strong as an ox," her father told her constantly.

"You're the next best thing to a boy. Pretty soon you be milking in the morning, too, when your sisters get a little older."

"Like that's something to get excited about," Margaret would say to herself every time he said it.

She got Annie settled in the highchair with blankets and tied her to the chair with a rope. Margaret fed her the porridge and a little milk as she sang a song she had secretly been working on when her parents were not around.

If I had a drum, I would pound out my pain,

and if I had a guitar, I would strum out in vain,

and then I would leave on a big red train,

away away to find a lovely home,

away away to find home sweet home.

Baby Annie smiled in between bites and hummed along with delight.

Margaret put Annie into her crib with some toys, and then headed over to the wash basin. She washed her face and brushed her long, curly red hair. She had decided never to cut it. Her mother's words still in her head: "You can keep it long, Margaret, but only if you take care of it and get the tangles out by yourself cuz I have no time for brushing everyone's hairs these days. I got enough to do." She was the only one in the family—except for baby Annie, who had no hair to speak of yet—that didn't have their father's famous "bowl cut." That is, short bangs that were rarely straight and no hair touching the shoulders. He used to make their hair real short with the small bowl, but her mother said the style at St. Mary's Catholic Church was ringlets for girls, and so he got a bigger bowl as his guide. Being the firstborn had some advantages, one being that the bowl cut only came after number three.

She had just turned five, and she remembered the day like it was yesterday. Her curly red hair was shoulder length, and when her father tried to cut it, she screamed and screamed, and then she ran around the house with her mother trying to catch her. "Like a cat chasing a mouse," her Ma would say when she would retell the story. Finally, her mother agreed that if she learned how to brush it herself, she could keep it long. That was all Margaret needed. She grabbed the brush and went to the mirror in the living room, and then practiced for an hour till there was not a tangle to be found.

That was one thing Margaret knew about herself: if someone told her to do something, she did it, and she did it well. Nobody had to explain things to her a second time. Aunt Beatrice told her that just last year, and she believed it to be true.

She went to the bedroom where her six sisters were sleeping. There were only two bedrooms in the farmhouse—one for her parents, who kept a crib where the latest baby slept, and another for all the rest of the kids. It was a wall of beds, so her father's rule was: "the one who goes to bed first goes to the farthest bed." As she was usually the first up and the last to go to bed because of her household duties, she was near the doorless doorway most times. The only time she slept between her identical twin sisters was when they were chatting too much or giggling. To get them to stop, she simply pushed them apart and stretched out between them. That gave them the message.

Baby Annie was already back to sleep. "Only took six songs this time," Margaret thought.

It was six thirty, time to get the rest of them up and help get them get dressed and ready for breakfast.

"Wake up. Rise and shine! Pull your socks over your head. It's time to get out of bed!"

She loved to come up with new rhymes or songs every morning when she woke up the girls. The book of nursery rhymes and children's songs that Aunt Beatrice had given her for Christmas was the best present she had ever received. Each day she would try out a new song or rhyme. The children seemed to love it, and they groaned less when it was time to go to bed or to get up in the morning. Most of her sisters were downright miserable in the mornings—and at bedtime, too—with the exception of quiet little Louise who never complained, and Helen, only ten months younger than Louise, who was as sweet as apple pie. Helen did have some fire in her though, and like Margaret, had a love for music. She had a beautiful voice and could sing harmony without anyone ever having taught her. In the mornings, Margaret often heard her humming and singing while the others were complaining.

"Come on, git those socks on and your faces washed. Porridge is ready."

As her sisters climbed out of bed, Margaret grabbed the potties from under the beds and bundled up in her coat, scarf, and winter boots, and headed outside to the outhouse. The cold wind hit her dead on and almost took her breath away. As she emptied the potties, she made a mental note to warm up the big rocks on the stove so they could use them to keep their feet warm on the buggy ride to school. "It is one of those days when the cold is enough to frost your eyeballs," Margaret thought.

She ran back inside the house and walked to the kitchen. She fed the sourdough starter with flour like she did every day so that her mother could bake bread after dinner. Her ma had told her how important it was to keep the sourdough fed so it wouldn't die off. She explained how the starter was a link to their ancestors and that it had been brought over on a boat from Ireland. She cut the homemade bread her mother had made the day before, filled a container with the sour cream that she had made herself, and put them both inside the school lunch buckets for herself and her twin sisters.

By the time her parents walked through the door, Margaret's sisters were sitting at the kitchen table, and Margaret was scooping porridge into the bowls. The smell of coffee filled the air; the fire in the stove had warmed up the kitchen; and the rocks were warming on top of the stove.

"Did ya say your prayers?" her father asked first thing.

"Yes, Father," they all said in unison.

"Good. Now, don't ya forget your prayers ever. God's listening at all times. Ya hear me?"

"Yeah, we hear," they answered.

"How can we forget?" Margaret thought to herself. "We pray nonstop! At church, before meals, then the rosary every evening after supper, and then again before going to bed. Jeez, I'd like to forget my bleedin' prayers, but you won't let me!"

As she listened to her father ramble on about praying, Margaret was reminded of a promise she had made to herself, and one which she had shared with her aunt.

"When I become a mother, I won't make my children pray at all. In fact, I might not even make them go to the Catholic church. I might go to a Protestant one like you and my grandparents, or maybe I won't go to church at all like the Dickson's who live two farms down. Father calls them "heathens" and says they will surely go to hell, but I think they are fine people and very generous and friendly, and they will probably go to heaven for being so nice. No, when I have children, instead of praying, I'll sing them silly songs and laugh and play with them."

"Margaret, don't worry too much about all that. When you get older you will figure out what is best," her aunt told her.

But she was pretty sure that she would keep that promise. Singing, laughing, and playing were all things her parents rarely did with any of them. It was work and pray, work and pray. They talked about sin all the time, but Margaret was as sure as the sun rising over the barn each morning that it was probably more sinful to never have any fun.

She glanced at the picture hanging above the stove as she poured her parents their coffee. It had praying hands that were carved out of wood, and underneath were the words: *The Family that Prays Together Stays Together.*

Margaret hated that saying, and she hated that picture. Every time she looked at it, she remembered her seventh birthday and the beating that kept her home from school for a week. Her father had beaten her right there in the kitchen in front of that stupid picture. In between punches, slaps, and kicks she would catch a glimpse of it and think, "I don't want to stay in this crazy family that *prays* together."

As she sat eating her porridge alone at the table after everyone was fed, her mind wandered back to one of her favourite days, the day she heard the radio interview of Bessie Smith. She was at Aunt Beatrice's house in Halifax. It was when Annie was born, and she had been sent there while the other children were sent to the houses of other relatives. She remembered the day as if it had happened yesterday. The two of them were sitting there in her living room. Her aunt was leaning forward in her big flowered armchair; She was sitting close to the radio on a purple velvet stool. She remembered her excitement as her aunt turned on the big, brown radio. Out came a man's clear deep voice. He was talking about their next guest.

"Miss Bessie Smith, the highest paid singer in the United States, is here with us today. Bessie, when did you start singing?"

"Well, to tell you the truth, I don't remember not singing at home—it was just what we did. My papa died before I really knew him, and then my mama died a few years later. So, at the age of nine my parents were both gone, and my sister Viola had to raise me and my two brothers. My brother Andrew and I busked on the streets in Chattanooga to make money. He played guitar, and I sang and danced. We were dirt poor."

"How did you get to be professional then?"

"Well, my older brother Clarence left home and starting singing with a troupe. When he returned home from a tour, he got me an audition. I was hired as a dancer, but I soon showed them I could sing! A man from Columbia Records discovered me when we were performing at a theatre right in Chattanooga where we lived. He heard me and approached me after the show, and he asked me to come sing for him and his partners in a recording studio. I didn't even really understand the significance of it till much later. I had my first hit in 1923, followed by a string of hits. The rest is history!"

"Well, Bessie, let's listen to "Ain't Nobody's Business.""

As they listened to the radio program, Margaret remembered being mesmerized. Occasionally she would look up at her aunt, and she would be smiling from ear to ear and looking like she was about to chuckle.

"Auntie, do you think I could be like Bessie Smith when I grow up? I mean get famous and make records and travel all over the United States and Canada?"

"Well, from what I can see, you have a real good chance at making it in the music business, Sweetie. I'd say you have voice of an angel and more rhythm in your baby finger than most people I know."

"I really want to be like Besse Smith, but I also want to play the guitar and write my own songs."

"Well, that sounds like quite an ambitious plan, Margaret. But you need to take some lessons and learn about singing, and playing a guitar, and writing music I would think. Do you know what kind of guitar you might like?"

"I don't know. I never saw one up real close before to know the difference between one or another."

"Well, let's look at the Sears Catalogue and see what they have, shall we?"

Aunt Beatrice got the Sears Catalogue out of the broom closet, and they sat at the kitchen table and looked through it together.

"Silverstone guitar, that's the one. Look! Can I cut it out? And show Ma?"

"Yes, of course, cut it out."

Margaret cut the page out. The picture was of a man on a chair with a brown Silverstone guitar on his lap. She folded the picture ever so gently and stuck it in her pocket.

How on earth would she tell her parents that she wanted the guitar? She thought and thought. Finally, she decided that she would ask on her birthday. It was in one month.

During that month, she took the picture out every day and carefully unfolded it and looked at it, imagining herself sitting on that same chair, holding the guitar and singing her own songs. By the time her seventh birthday rolled around, the picture was worn and creased.

She served her parents their after-breakfast coffee, then took the picture of the guitar out, and with her little hands shaking, she set it on the table in front of them. And as she had rehearsed in her head so many times in the last month, she carefully said: "Mother. Father. It is my birthday today, and I was wondering if I could please get a guitar and singing lessons so that I can become a famous singer. I'll work extra hard and won't miss doing any of my chores, I promise!"

Her mother looked at her with wide and fearful eyes, a look that Margaret recognized only too well, and then her mother hid her face in her hands. Margaret's mother seemed to always know when her husband's foul mood meant that someone was going to get a beating to remember, and Margaret had learned to look for her mother's cues. But she had been concentrating so much on her request that she missed her mother's warning signs. Too late. Without missing a beat, her father jumped up from the table and backhanded her face so hard that she flew across the room, her head just missing the stove by a sliver.

"You don't deserve anything let alone a guitar or singing lessons, ungrateful little turd." He screamed. He kicked her in the ribs with his boot. "You're nothin' special. You're just a big kid built like an ox who's only good for workin'."

Holding her ribs, she tried to get up off the floor, but she was too slow. He grabbed her braids and dragged her to the doorway where the belt was hanging, then he grabbed her foot and twisted it until her body turned and she was face down on the floor. He hit her bottom and back with the belt, all the time screaming at her: "Ungrateful wench, lucky ya had clothes and food in your belly. What makes ya think you are so special that ya deserve a guitar? You're nothin' special. Did ya think money grows on trees?"

Throughout the whole beating, the praying hands picture above the stove flashed before her eyes.

It was late spring, her favourite time of year, but on that day as she lay on her bed moaning from the pain, she was anything but excited. Her right eye was swollen completely shut, and she was sure she had more than one broken rib. She wanted to cry, but when she did, the pain was worse. Every breath brought excruciating pain. There was not an inch of her body that did not ache and throb.

The window to the bedroom was open, and she watched the clouds pass by and tried to bring her attention to the fresh smell of spring. A tree branch with fresh young leaves was visible from her bed, and every so often a black-capped chickadee landed on it. Margaret loved listening to the chickadees sing; distinguishing the different songs they sang depending on if they were mating, or defending their young, or warning others of danger. It fascinated her. But on this day, it was not the sound of the chickadee that she noticed; it was how these beautiful birds could just fly and go wherever they wanted. More than anything, she wished in that moment that she could fly; fly away from the farm, her father, and her life. She imagined all the places she would go: her aunt's house, maybe to other provinces, or even other countries.

She closed her eyes, and as she drifted off, she could feel her body lifting off the ground, her arms spread out wide, soaring above the farm, then over her aunt's house in Halifax, then higher and higher till she was flying so high she could see the oceans, and mountains, and cities, and farm lands, and fields of purple. She felt the wind supporting her, guiding her to places she had only seen in books.

She awoke to pain, tears running down her face. There was a world to see, and she realized then, in that moment, that she had to change her ways if she wanted to live. That was when she made a promise to herself. "I promise not to ask for anything or let anyone know my hopes and dreams. If I want to live, I have to keep my mouth shut. That way I won't get a beating. If I don't, he might kill me sure enough."

Six months later...

It worked! For the past six months, her parents had started calling her their "little nun." She was not sure she liked the nickname, but at least the beatings had stopped. She still had her hopes and dreams about becoming a famous singer and songwriter, but she made sure to keep them to herself. "When I get older and leave home, I can do what I want. That is what Aunt Beatrice told me, and I believe her," she thought.

1928-1931

The one-room school house was Margaret's favourite place. She loved the smell of the books, the chalk, and of the smoke from the wood burning stove. Her teacher Mrs. McDonald always had the room warmed up and greeted her pupils with a smile. She would help the little ones with their coats, and whenever she walked by you, she would place her hand on your shoulder or pat your head and say what a good job you were doing. She never raised her voice—unless the boys were having a fist fight outside. She was always dressed in plain, clean clothes, and her hair was always in the same bun. Mrs. McDonald was older than Margaret's parents, and her children were already finished school, but she often daydreamed what it would be like to have her for a mother.

"Margaret, will you help the younger ones with their spelling?" Mrs. McDonald asked.

"Oh, yes, Ma'am, I'd love to help."

The children gathered around Margaret, and a little boy named Jake slipped his tiny hand into hers and looked up at her with loving eyes. He was the youngest in the class, and she was one of the senior students despite being only eleven. She lifted him up, sat him on her knee, and opened the book.

"Okay! Every time you spell a word correctly, you have to sing a verse from a song with the word in it."

"T O P," screamed Paul.

"Very good! Okay, what is a song with the word TOP in it?"

Harry, began to sing, "On Top of Ole Smokey, all covered in snow..."

"Yes, very good!" she said and clapped her hands.

Margaret noticed Mrs. McDonald looking over at her, smiling and nodding as she stoked the wood stove at the back of the schoolhouse. She couldn't help but love her teacher. She never asked questions about her bruises or limping, but Margaret could tell by the look in her eyes that Mrs. McDonald knew when she was in pain, and she was always extra kind to her on those days; days like today. Her eye was swollen and green and yellow, but Mrs. McDonald never asked what happened. She would just say things like, "I am here for you if you want to talk," or do small things like make an ice pack from the ice in the ice box and put it on her swollen shoulder during recess, or bandage an open wound. It was a relief not to have to make up new excuses for her beatings. How many times can you say you tripped and fell without sounding like a real klutz?

When lunchtime was over, Margaret grabbed the baseball and the bat and ran outside. "Who wants to play ball?"

There was no shortage of players. Within minutes they had a game going, and Margaret was smiling from ear to ear. She knew she was not the greatest at playing ball, but it didn't matter. She loved the feel of the sun on her face as she ran, and she laughed out loud when she was batting, even when she was striking out.

"We will begin rehearsals for the fall school play." Mrs. McDonald said later. "This year we are doing *The Princess and The Pea*. We have made it into a musical. Margaret, you will be the Princess. My husband, Mr. McDonald, whom you are all familiar with, has picked out the songs, and he will play the guitar, along with Mrs. McGuire, who will play piano."

Margaret smiled, jumped up from her desk, and went to the front of the class.

Mrs. McDonald named off the rest of the cast and handed them their booklets.

"The rest of you, come with me. We need to plan what props to build for our play."

The class was buzzing with excitement; Margaret's first thought was, "I need to let Aunt Beatrice know so she can plan to come."

She knew her parents would never come; they never did. But Aunt Beatrice never missed Margaret's school plays. She rode her horse and buggy from Halifax by herself through rain and snow to see Margaret perform. Once Margaret wrote an essay about what it felt like to be around her aunt, and she got an A++ from Mrs. McDonald.

Seeing my aunt is like when the sun explodes between the clouds on a cloudy day and you feel warm and safe—like a sigh of relief. She is like the sweet taste of a fresh baby carrot that you steal from the garden while you're weeding. She is like the earthy sweet smell of freshly cut hay. She is like the boost of energy all over your body when you go outside after the rain has stopped. She is like the music you hear on the radio that makes your insides feel like they are dancing. She is like the calm when you're alone outside at night and you hear the crickets singing to the stars as they do their twinkly dance. There is no one who can even come close to my aunt Beatrice.

Beside the bright red *A++* on the top of the page, Mrs. McDonald wrote: *Margaret, this essay sounds like it would be a good inspiration for a song! Excellent job!*

On the morning of September 5, 1930, Margaret, now twelve, was making school lunches for her and her sisters. She was cutting the tomatoes she had just picked from the garden when her father walked into the kitchen and told her that she was done with school.

"Grade six, that's enough. That's three more years than I ever had. Look at your mother. She had eight, and she ain't no better than me. Nova Scotia is in bad times. We ain't had rain, and the crops are failing but everyone still needs milk, and we're lucky that we got a deep lake on our land and have saved enough feed over the years that we'll survive longer than most farmers. We're getting ten more cows from the Millers up the road tomorrow. They can't afford to feed them anymore. I got a good deal. Don't know where they will go with all those kids and being they's as poor as church mice. Someone said Paul was starting a moonshine business, but that might just be talk. Anyway, I'll be needin' you to work in the barn, Ox. The others are old enough to run the household now. And right now, we got a calf comin', and I need those strong arms of yours. Now get goin'."

Margaret was about to open her mouth in protest, "But..."

He was watching her with his green hawk eyes, and when her mouth opened, he raised his fist.

"Don't you dare, Ox, who's the father here? Get to the barn now!"

Margaret was five foot, ten inches with strong long legs. She could outrun her father. She knew that for sure. Without hesitation, she turned and ran out of the house to the barn, but not to where the cows were. She climbed up to the hayloft and threw herself onto the bales in the far corner where the baby kittens slept. Her heart beat hard and fast, and tears welled up in her eyes. She held her chest and doubled over and sobbed, her body heaving back and forth like a giant wave. "No, No, oh, please, God, if you do exist, please don't let him do this to me! Please, please."

After what seemed like an hour of crying, she fell silent. The kittens were whimpering, and their mother looked at her, then came over and rubbed against her legs and purred. Margaret stroked her gently and silently whispered, "Thank you."

Margaret watched as the mother cat stretched out on her side and the kittens attached to her nipples and started to nurse, kneading her bare belly with their paws as they suckled. The mother purred low and steady while keeping her eyes locked on Margaret's. She saw love in that cat's eyes that she had never noticed before. Love for her kittens, but love for her, too. She felt the love. Suddenly, her anger was gone, and she felt so sad.

She wondered why her own mother never came to check on her. "She doesn't love me, that's why," she told herself.

She heard her father in the barn below, grunting and swearing, and she heard Daisy the cow bawling like she had never heard a cow bawl before. Margaret climbed down the ladder and went to the stall where Daisy was trying to give birth to a breeched calf. She got there just in time to get her hands inside and turn the baby while her father pulled the calf out. Margaret had been to enough births to know there was way too much blood. Daisy's cries became weaker and weaker, and then finally stopped altogether. Margaret saw her big brown eyes cease moving. She imagined her own self dead, laying on the wooden floor of the barn with her eyes staring into nothing, just like poor Daisy.

She imagined it would be peaceful. There'd be no pain; no suffering; no screaming; no tears; no beatings.

With tear-stained cheeks, she helped her father drag Daisy out into the yard. They grabbed two shovels and together they dug a large hole. Margaret took an old broken fence post and used it to push Daisy into the hole. Then she and her father shoveled dirt till the cow was covered up. There were no words spoken between them.

Back at the barn, Margaret found a large bottle with a nipple, filled it with cow's milk from the milk pail, and cradled the tiny calf in her arms, singing lullabies as she fed her.

"Lovey, that is your name," she said to the calf as she stroked her head.

When she finally crawled into bed that night she fought to sleep, her head swirling with thoughts of how she would ever survive if she couldn't go to school, mixed with images of Daisy's eyes staring straight ahead. She decided she hated her parents, the farm, the beatings, everything. Her last thought before drifting off to sleep was, "I'm better off dead."

The following month, Margaret saw Auntie Beatrice in Halifax. She had hired her to help her clean up her yard for the fall. Margaret told her aunt she wanted to die.

"Margaret, you will not die. You will survive, and I'll help you. It is a crying shame that they won't let you go to school anymore, but Margaret, you're going to have to live with it. I'll bring you homework every week, and I'll make sure you're getting what you need to stay ahead in school. You're lucky that I'm a teacher. I'll make sure you're keeping up. Where there is a will, there is a way, child. Always remember that."

Beatrice waited for Margaret to say something, but she made no sound. She sighed and lifted her arms in the air.

"I know you will miss school, and the plays, and your teacher, but you must pull up your socks and get on with it."

Margaret still didn't respond. She worked in silence, raking the dead leaves.

As the years passed, Margaret used a scribbler that Aunt Beatrice gave her to keep a diary.

June 21, 1931

Dear Diary,

Today is my fourteenth birthday. I have to write to you, as I have no one else to talk to. My beloved Lovey died yesterday. She was my everything since her mother died giving birth to her. She followed me around every day and waited for me at the door every morning to come outside. We didn't even need to put her behind a fence. She was my best friend who I told all my secrets to. The vet said she had blackleg disease from not getting enough colostrum on a count of when her mother died, and she didn't get that special milk that baby calves need. I know it's crazy, but I feel so alone in a household with eleven siblings and my parents. It's as if they don't see me as a person with feelings, wants, or desires. My parents just work, and say the rosary, and yell out orders to me as if I was their slave. Last week I got what I hope was my last whooping. Father was angry because I had menstruation pain and couldn't go to the barn and milk. Ma told him I needed to rest with a hot water bottle. I heard her talk to him in the kitchen. For once my mother was standing up for me. What a shock that was! The cramps were so bad, I even fainted in the kitchen. That was when Ma insisted that I go to bed, and she brought me a hot water bottle and some willow bark to chew on for the pain. Father came into my room and slapped me hard across the face, then told me to get up. Ma screamed at him to leave me alone. Miraculously, he left. I wonder if now that I'm a woman, he will stop the beatings. I hope so. I miss school so much, and I hate working on the farm all day long and looking after the children. I wish there was a way I could leave, but Auntie says I have to wait till I'm over sixteen, then I'll be mature enough to leave this place. That is two years away! I don't think I can stand it. I wish I was dead. It would be better than this life.

Thank you, diary, for listening.

Love, Margaret

Aunt Beatrice had requested hiring Margaret to help with spring cleaning, and as long as Beatrice paid her father in person, he usually agreed with her requests. The fact that her husband had disappeared after one year of marriage played in their favour, she had explained to Margaret many times growing up.

"It makes me look helpless."

Little did he know that there was often no work to be done, and they would just spend the time together.

He dropped her off on his way to deliver milk to the train station.

Margaret knocked on the door. She heard Aunt Beatrice yelling, "Margaret, you're here!" She opened the door. "Come in, come in!" She grabbed Margaret's hand and pulled her into the living room so fast that she could hardly get her shoes off. "I have something I'm sure you're going to love!"

"You know just being here with you is what I love!"

"Sit down, child."

Margaret sat down on the edge of her favourite purple stool and watched her aunt run into the bedroom. "What on earth was she was so excited about?" Margaret wondered.

Beatrice came out of the bedroom with a blue guitar in one hand and a bag of books in the other.

Margaret's eyes lit up, and she let out a yelp. "Holy Liftin' Dina! Is that for me?" Beatrice grabbed a card from the dining room table and handed it to Margaret.

"Read the card first, Margaret."

She opened the card and instantly recognized the handwriting.

"It's from my teacher, Mrs. McDonald!"

Dearest Margaret,

I can't tell you how I have missed you! You were always a ray of sunshine in our school, and we have all missed you terribly.

As you probably heard, my beloved husband of thirty years passed away from an accident at the coal mine. It has been a terrible time. I do miss him a great deal. He was a good, quiet man. The only thing he loved to do in his spare time was play the guitar and sing.

He taught himself with books he ordered from the Sears Catalogue. When he died, I immediately thought of you when I looked at his guitar, which he loved so much. He would be thrilled that it got passed on to you. He heard many stories about you and how you loved music and made-up songs, many of which I tried to sing to him when I would come home from school. Of course, as you know, I'm a little tone deaf, so we always had a good laugh. But he would always say, "Now that girl has talent. Writing songs at her age, she will go far with her music." We were both devastated for you when you had to quit school. He was particularly angry, as he never had an education, and so he made sure that all his children went to college and that I became a teacher, like I so wanted to be. He never complained about working at the coal mine because, he said, it paid the bills, but he hoped that none of his children would have to work there. He believed education was so important. He was a smart man, and alongside the children, he learned how to read, and write, and do arithmetic, and then later on, he taught himself how to play the guitar. There was no stopping him if he put his mind to something. A quality I see in you, dear Margaret. Please keep in touch, and I hope you live out all your dreams and that I will see you play your guitar and sing one day. That would give me such great pleasure.

With admiration, your teacher and friend,

Mrs. Edna McDonald

Margaret looked up to see her aunt's eyes tearing up.

"She thought it was best to have me give it to you, as she was afraid of what your father might do if she brought the guitar out to the farm," she explained.

Margaret felt the weirdest sensation—a feeling of sadness for her teacher mixed with a joy so profound that she felt she could burst into dance. She began to cry and laugh at the same time as she jumped around the room and kissed and hugged her aunt.

Margaret spent the next two days with the guitar on her lap and the books spread out on the dining room table.

"Margaret, time to eat. You've got to stop for a few minutes."

"Just one more minute. I almost have this cord figured out. Wanna see?"

Later the next evening as Margaret and Beatrice sat in the living room in their nighties, Margaret finally asked the question that had lingered on both their minds for the last two days.

"How can I take this guitar home? Do I hide it? Or do I even tell my parents? Should I leave it here to play when I come? What should I do?"

1933

The night before Margaret's sixteenth birthday was a Saturday, and it was bath day. She got the washtubs out of the cellar and put the water to boil on the stove. The older twins helped her get the littlest ones in the tubs, then she washed them with the last of the homemade lye soap they had made last year, and the twins rinsed them off with buckets. One by one, from youngest to oldest, all eleven were bathed. When it was her turn, she checked and rechecked to make sure no one was around. She covered herself with a towel till she got in the washtub. Listening for her father's voice, she quickly washed, then grabbed the towel from the stool, dried herself, and slipped her nightgown over her head.

"I'm done," she yelled out as she put her robe on over her nightgown.

Her mother walked in and said, "I've done the ringlets on the older girls. Can you do the last four while I have my bath?"

"Sure, Ma."

She went into the living room and called the girls in one by one, instructing them to sit on the little wooden stool.

She took the rags from the basket and curled the girls' hair.

"Can you sing me that song, Margaret, the one about the dancing chickens?" asked Rachael.

"You like that one? I'm still working on it. I think I need to change the verse. Tell me which one you like better."

Just as she was about to start singing, her mother yelled out: "Margaret, make sure you do your own hair in braids, and don't just leave it wild like you always do. You want to look your best Monday morning."

"Monday morning?" She wondered what was so important about looking her best on Monday morning?

When her mother came into the living room a few minutes later, Margaret asked, "What are you talkin' bout, Ma? What's so special about Monday?"

"You're off to the convent, you know that. We have talked about it before."

"I told you, Ma, I ain't going to no convent to be a Catholic nun. I never agreed to that. I don't want to go to the convent, and I for sure ain't going to be some nun." Her voice raised an octave as she looked her mother directly in the eye.

"It ain't up to you. It's your destiny as first born."

"I ain't goin. You can't make me! And, besides, who will do all the work around here if I go?"

"Keep your voice down! Yous going and not another word."

Margaret's chest tightened, a burning wave raced up her throat, and her face grew hot. She noticed that her mother's hands were trembling and that her face had that frightened look, a look Margaret knew all too well. It was the warning sign, the plea to calm down because her father was in one of his moods

Anger heaved up from deep inside her body. She ran to the bedroom and pressed a pillow over her face, then screamed into it and pounded the mattress, "I'm not going to become a prisoner in a convent. I refuse!"

That night she tossed and turned, and her mind raced from thoughts of escaping in the night, to figuring out ways to try and explain to her parents so they would listen, to thinking that perhaps the convent would at least be better than this life. By morning, she decided she would take her chance and go to the convent. She was counting the days until she could leave the farm anyway. Aunt Beatrice had said that after she was sixteen or seventeen, she would be mature enough to leave. But what finally convinced Margaret was an imaginary scenario with her explaining her situation to Mother Superior, who then responded by saying, "You poor dear. You do not have to be a nun. How can we help you?"

"Surely, a nun who was so close to God wouldn't force her to become one if it was not her calling," she decided.

Her mother prepared all her favourite foods for her birthday/farewell supper: tarragon chicken, potatoes with parsnips mashed together with dill, fresh creamed peas, and wild blueberry upside down cake with fresh whipped cream. After supper, she and her sisters went to the yard and played "kick the can" till the sun began to set.

"Time to come in!" her mother yelled.

"I'll be a few more minutes. You kids get in the house and get ready for bed. I'll come in a bit and sing you a song before you go to bed. Off you go now," she said as she shooed them into the house.

Margaret walked over to the gardens and gazed at the rows and rows of vegetables. She picked the purple flowers off the chives and took the pea plants that were laying down and attached them to the trellis. Two kittens purred at her feet.

"Oh, my little sweethearts, come here," she said as she picked up the kittens. She rubbed their heads, necks, and ears, and they purred even louder, closing their eyes in ecstasy. She held them as she walked to the pasture gate and gazed out at the cows. Some were grazing on the grass, and some were laying peacefully under the moonlit sky. Then she walked to the chicken coop and gathered the flock into the enclosure for the night before heading for the house. In the distance, she could see her father driving the pickup truck with fence posts and wire hanging out the back. She hurried to the house, hoping to avoid him—for sure he would find more work for her to do before bed.

She looked at her eleven siblings sprawled across the beds. It was a sea of red curly hair and freckled bodies amid the blankets and pillows. All of Margaret's siblings were girls except the youngest two, who were twin boys, now tucked in between the oldest twins, Mary and Rachael.

"Now listen up. This is the last time I'll sing you to sleep because I'm leaving tomorrow for the convent in Halifax. So quiet now."

Louise lifted up little two-year-old Harriet and came and sat right in front of Margaret.

Margaret noticed that Louise had tears in her eyes but she said nothing to her. That was her way. "She is such a quiet thing," Margaret thought as she looked into her eyes. She often wondered whether this was because she was scared, or because she was brave.

She wasn't quite sure of all the words to the song yet, but the melody was catchy and she thought the words were appropriate, given the circumstances.

"Grab your coat and get your hat, leave your worries on the doorstep, life can be so sweet, on the sunny side of the street."

It was sung by Ted Lewis whom she had never heard of before.

She heard her mother humming along quietly from the living room as she sang.

It was 1933, and the songs on the radio were often war songs, but she liked them anyway. She liked to listen to the guitars and try and figure out the chords they were playing, and then she would get out her *How to Play Guitar* book from under her mattress and practice the chords on a piece of wood she used to mimic the frets on a guitar. She had made two wooden guitars, one she kept under the bed, and the other in the hayloft.

Her favourite radio show was a weekly program called *Station Aunt* with Mary Helen Creighton who played folk songs from the Maritimes. Luckily, it seemed to come on when her father was in the barn.

"I wonder if they have a radio at the convent? Will they let me go to Aunt Beatrice's house to visit so I can play my guitar? Maybe I can bring the guitar to the convent?" she thought.

It was hard to sleep. There were so many thoughts going through her head. Who would take her place? Mary and Rachael, God love them, were next in line. Fourteen and a half years old, but they were so lazy and barely able to do a thing without being instructed over and over. She was sure they were simple minded, or at least that is what she overheard her mother and aunt discussing once. Maybe Louise, who was thirteen, and quiet but a good worker. She was pretty strong, but she wasn't tall. In fact, none of her sibling were tall like her, not yet anyway. Louise seemed to be the only one who avoided their father's wrath altogether when she thought about it. "Yes, it will probably be Louise," she murmured aloud.

On Monday morning, the day after her sixteenth birthday, her mother took her by the hand when no one was around and guided her to the bedroom.

"Margaret, I have something for you for your birthday but it is to be a secret. Understand?"

"Yes, Ma, what is it? she said with a hint of excitement.

Her mother took a tiny rectangular box out of her dresser and handed it to her.

"What is it, Ma?"

"This is a harmonica that your father got from his father—your Grampie Andrew, who you never met. You may find it hard to believe but your father loved to play music and sing when he was a small boy, much like his father before him. He was the second child and when he was nine years of age, *his* father died by being crushed by a bull in the barn. His mother, your Granny Irene, quickly remarried a man called Eddie, a widower with two children from the next town, and they went on to have seven more children."

"You mean Grampie Eddie is not my real Grampie?"

"Yes, I know your father never wanted to talk about it much. But from what little he told me, and from stories I've heard, his birth father was a nice man, loved to sing and play music, who worked hard but always had a smile on his face. Then, after he died and his mother married Eddie, their life changed drastically. Grampie Eddie was a strong Catholic, and he believed that the only music worthy of singing were Catholic hymns. He never allowed your father to play his harmonica or sing the songs he grew up singing with his father. He was a very strict man, and when we were courting, your father told me stories of being beaten and left in a dark damp cellar for days as punishment. I felt so sorry for him when he told me these stories. It broke my heart. I found this harmonica hidden in a box in the cellar a few years ago, and when I asked him about it, he said it was a piece of junk, and he grabbed it and threw it in the garbage. He doesn't know that I took it out of the garbage and hid it, hoping that one day he might want to play it again. But then last night I realized that perhaps it was meant for you and not for him. You're the only one in this family who has a love of music besides Helen, but she just loves singing, and you seem to have a talent for writing, singing, and playing the guitar. Yes, your aunt told me the whole story about the guitar. So, I want you to take it. I don't know if your father had any actual musical talent cause I never heard him sing or nothin'. But I do know that you have a talent, and it is a God-given talent, child, and I hope you pursue it somehow. I only ask that you never play it around your father because I don't know how he would react."

"Ma, I don't know what to say. I'll cherish it, and I promise not to let Father know I have it. But, Ma, I don't understand. If you believe I have talent, how can I become a famous singer and performer if I'm in the convent?" she said, her voice rising.

"Margaret, I don't know what your future holds. But I have no say in you going to the convent. It's what Catholics do. Your father's oldest brother is a priest, and most families have their first born serve the church. Personally, I thought Louise would have made a better nun, but your father insisted you go. I have no say, you know that, Margaret. The man is the head of the house, and that is something you have to get through your head or you're going to have a hard time finding your place in this world. Now get going, child, you're leaving in a few minutes. I don't want your father to be waiting."

Margaret packed up her little bag, hiding her wooden play guitar on the bottom along with the harmonica, and then she slid her diary and guitar book under her clothing and bid farewell to her family.

"Now we be talking soon. Mind your p's and q's," her mother said as her limp hand touched her back.

It was almost funny how her mother seemed to change once she was within earshot of her husband. A few minutes ago, she had felt closer to her mother than she ever remembered, and now she was back to her regular, distant, uncaring self.

"She is not like Aunt Beatrice at all," Margaret thought. "Auntie Bea's hugs are amazing! You can feel her whole body and her arms wrap right around you and more often than not, the hugs end with a nice kiss on the cheek or forehead. Hard to believe they came from the same family."

She stood there looking at her siblings all lined up. Some of them were crying; some of them were too young to know what was happening. She went up to each one of them and hugged them and kissed them one last time, and she told them how special they were and that she would never forget them.

"Let's git going, Ox, times is ticking," her father yelled from the truck.

She climbed in, and then she turned her head and watched as her family and the farm became smaller and smaller till the truck turned a corner and they were gone.

Her father took her to Sisters of Mercy Convent in Halifax, and dropped her off as if it was the most normal thing in the world to do.

"Get going now. I ain't got all day. And don't forget to say the rosary every day."

"Geez, is he kidding? I'm going into a bloody convent," she said to herself.

He never got out of the truck, or gave her a hug, or walked her to the door.

Margaret thought: "Well, I won't be missing him any time soon."

Margaret had a strange feeling as she walked up the stairs to the convent. She had seen the convent many times before when she went for first communion and confirmation lessons, but it looked different now somehow. The red bricks seemed brighter and the ivy clinging to the bricks looked like a lace decoration. The window frames were bright white, and she could see white curtains blowing gently out of the windows like angel wings, so calm and soft. She saw the giant white front door with a large brass knocker that hung from a cross with pretty swirls engraved on it. She grabbed hold of the cross and banged it gently against the door.

The door opened immediately, as if the person on the other side had been standing there waiting for her arrival.

A petite young nun stood there with a wide smile that showed her gums and her teeth that were so tiny they looked like they were still her baby teeth. She looked like she was not much older than Margaret was.

"Welcome, you must be Margaret!" Not waiting for a reply, she added: "I'm Sister Denis. Come in."

Margaret followed the nun inside and tried to follow her small steps, but it was difficult because one of her steps equalled three of Sister Denis's. She noticed how clean and shiny everything was—the walls and the floors literally sparkled. The tiled floors under her feet made their steps echo in the quiet halls. Loud clump then three tiny little clumps. The building felt cold, and there was a strong, odd smell of disinfectant mixed with frankincense. When she was shown her small, sterile room, Margaret almost giggled.

"My own room!"

She touched the back of her dress and felt her diary and guitar book still tucked under her clothes. Her first thought was: "I can read and write my music without having to find a place to hide."

She had privacy for the first time in her life.

"No cows, no children, no parents, maybe it won't be so bad after all," she thought.

"This is your room, Margaret. There is a uniform in the closet for you to put on. Supper is in two hours. You will hear the bell."

"Thank you, Sister Denis."

Margaret laid down on her tiny wooden bed. At six feet tall, her feet hung off the end by almost a foot, but it was the most magnificent bed she had ever known—and it was her own! Except for when she stayed at her aunt's house (where she slept in the guest room), she had never had her own bed. She gazed out the window at the tall buildings and the city sprawled out before her. She could almost see her aunt's house. Then Margaret looked around the grounds of the convent and saw some sisters in their black habits watering the flowers and the garden, and others holding their rosaries, walking slowly along the path alone, leaving space between them as if they measured it so that they were all the exactly the same length apart.

She grinned as she thought about how they looked like little ducklings walking in a row.

She unpacked her bag, hung up her clothes, and put on her blue novice uniform, safely tucking her diary under her clothes. She pinned up her long red braids so they were not visible under the head dress. Or so she thought. There were no mirrors in the room. The only thing that hung on the walls was one plain wooden cross above her bed, a cross that didn't even have Jesus on it.

After supper she went to her room and grabbed her diary out of her underpants, took her pencil out of her desk drawer, and began to write.

Dear Diary,

I have my own room! Sister Denis showed me the grounds, the kitchen, the laundry, and of course, the chapel. Everything is so clean and orderly. She told me I'll start working in the laundry tomorrow. At five o'clock the bell rang, and I went to eat supper. There was a prayer led by Mother Superior, and then we were served a very bland and tasteless bowl of pea soup and some dry bread that was clearly missing salt. I would like to see if I can grow an herb garden and maybe work in the kitchen instead of the laundry. It is obvious they don't know how to cook with flavours. But saying that, I hope I don't have to stay too long. I had a brief meeting with Mother Superior who seems like a grouchy, unhappy old woman. She made it clear she wants me to be a nun. I was going to say something, but she "dismissed" me and waved her hand. I'm sure she had orders from Father! But I'm confident that in time I can find a way out. I mean, being a nun is the MOST unappealing job I can think of. Just watching them makes me bored silly. I wanted to ask if I could call Aunt Beatrice to come visit me or if I am allowed to have anyone visit me. I feel like I may enjoy the solitude eventually, but I do miss my sisters a little. I have to be patient. I'm sure I can have a better conversation later on with Mother Superior. Let's hope anyway, or I'll go crazy, especially if I can't see Auntie Beatrice or play my guitar again.

Love, Margaret

As Margaret walked around the grounds in her free hour, she began to sing and swing her hips to the Duke Ellington song "It Don't Mean a Thing if it Ain't Got that Swing." She could hear the big band and piano in her mind as she sang and made trumpet noises with her lips for the solo parts. She didn't notice the sisters watching her.

At home, Margaret was rarely praised. The odd time, her mother said she was a good worker, and her father's only comments were about her brute strength. But at the convent she couldn't do anything right, and she was constantly in trouble for talking out of turn, making sounds while eating, singing non-Catholic songs on the grounds, even going to the kitchen to help when it was not her turn.

She was used to being in charge at home, but at the convent she was not allowed to make decisions. She was told what to do, when to do it, and how to do it, and with absolutely no questions asked. She learned that the hard way, one week into her stay, when Mother Superior told her she was not allowed to sing songs in her free time on the grounds.

"But why, Mother Superior?"

"Why, you ask why? Because it is heathen music!" she screamed. Then she was sent to her room with no supper.

Another time, she was sitting in the dining room trying to eat the watered-down porridge, but it was so bland. She was moving it around in her bowl hoping to make it look like she was eating, when Mother Superior came up to her.

"Stand up, Margaret McLean."

Margaret noticed the scowl on her face. She stood up, and then looked down at Mother Superior, as she was at least a foot taller. She wondered what it was she wanted. Then she saw her take two wooden clothes pins out of her pocket. She held them up, and then she pinned them to her ears.

A hush came over the dining hall, and Margaret heard gasps from some of the sisters in the room. Stunned, Margaret just stood there speechless.

"These pins are to remind you, Missy, that the Lord has no ears for heathen music!" Mother Superior said in a very loud voice, and then she turned abruptly, clicked her heels, and walked away.

Margaret stood there for what seemed an eternity, and then slowly walked out of the dining hall and back to her room.

Dear Diary,

It has been three months in this hell hole. What a joke! Sisters of Mercy? Mercy? As if! They are so mean. Wearing clothes pins on my ears for a week was bad enough, but I can't even sing what I want. I must obey, obey, obey. I must be silent for hours on end and pray day and night—on top of saying the rosary twice a day. I have no desire what-so-ever of becoming a nun, but when I told Mother Superior, she said to be patient and the desire would come. She asked me if I believed in the Trinity, and I said 'not really.' She did not like that. She said I need to spend more time in silence so I can connect with God. I had to wear a sign around my neck for three days that said I'm in silence, and so no one talked to me or even looked at me! Only one nun, Sister Denis, smiled at me once when no one was looking. I have been planning my escape for weeks.

Tonight, I leave. I refuse to cry myself to sleep one more night. I want to pursue my own dreams, not my father's dream.

Wish me luck!

Love, Margaret

When the lights went out just before midnight, Margaret dressed herself under the sheets, slipped her diary and guitar book under her clothes, put the harmonica in her pocket, and then snuck out of the building and into the garden. She crawled under the fence, which was not an easy feat. She thanked the nuns under her breath for their terrible cooking because the weight she lost in the last three months helped her slip her six-foot frame just under the fence.

Margaret looked down at her dress; she was covered in dirt. But she didn't waste any time cleaning herself off. She needed to get to her aunt's, and she knew it wasn't too far from the convent. She began to run, and she didn't stop until she saw the little blue and white house that looked like a dollhouse in a magazine. Aunt Beatrice had the loveliest flower and herb gardens; it was no wonder that she won first prize almost every year for the most beautiful yard in Halifax. The house was small, and there was not a blade of grass to be found. Instead, there were flowers and herbs of every colour and shape. She had taught herself how to cross pollinate and every year people would ask her for her seeds, which she happily shared.

She knocked on the door. As she waited for her aunt to come to the door, she remembered the many times that she had come to stay at her house. They would do a little work, but they always made time to sing, dance to the radio, and go shopping downtown. Later, when Margaret got her guitar, she would practice and try and put the songs she wrote to music. They always tried to go to the Ceilidh at the church basement near her house, and people would sing and dance and play east coast music, so long as Margaret promised not to tell her parents or her siblings—which of course she never did. Her father would never allow her to come to her aunt's house if he knew they were going out and having fun. It was about work—and only work. He told her time and again that music on the radio was the *work of the devil*. She wasn't sure what he might do if he knew she was out and about going to Ceilidhs, but she knew deep down that it would probably mean a beating and the refusal to let her come to her aunt's place ever again.

Margaret knocked again loudly on the door of her aunt's house. Her breathing slowed down. Although it was cool outside for July, the sweat dripped off her face. Finally, after what seemed like an hour, she heard her aunt coming down the stairs.

"Who's there at this time of night?"

"Auntie, it's me, Margaret."

The door opened. There stood Aunt Beatrice in her flannel nightgown. She had the same flaming red hair that she and Margaret's mother had and tonight it was braided in one long thick braid that nearly touched her waist. Like Margaret's mother, she was only five foot two, but besides the colour of their hair and their height, they looked nothing alike. Auntie Beatrice had the most beautiful porcelain skin, and her bright green eyes seemed to look into your soul. Margaret noticed that even without her makeup she looked beautiful. She was a year younger than her own mother, but in appearance, she was even more youthful. Her mother had grey hair, a rugged complexion, pursed lips, and heavy lines on her forehead. "Probably from frowning so much," she thought. Aunt Beatrice had no wrinkles what-so-ever and not a single grey hair.

"Sweetie, what are you doing here? Why are you full of dirt?"

"Please, Auntie, I can't go back there! Don't make me."

"Come in, sit down, and I'll make you a cup of tea."

"Please don't call my parents. I don't want to go back home either."

In her usual calm voice, she said, "What do you plan on doing then?"

"I'll get a job here in Halifax. I can live here and help you."

"Sweetie, when you were a baby, there was nothing more I wanted than to have you as my child. You were the best thing that ever happened to me. If you had not come into my life, I don't know how I would have ever gotten over my depression that overcame me when George walked out on me. God, it was a terrible time in my life. I'm going to tell you a little story that I think will help you."

Margaret looked at her aunt. She loved hearing her stories, but she wondered how one could help her in this predicament.

"I felt so dead inside, so lost, ashamed and terrified when my husband, my best friend, walked out on me. But then one day, while sitting in my chair in the living room, I had a realization that me, Beatrice, was still inside me. It was like a tiny seed in the middle of my chest. A teeny, tiny Beatrice seed that was so full of goodness and just waiting to be nourished so it could come back to life. From that day on, I would sit quietly and ask my seed what it wanted me to do. And that began my journey to heal. It needed food, okay, I made it something to eat. It wanted to breathe the ocean air, okay, I took it out for a walk by the ocean. It needed the warmth of a hug, so I would ask Mary to bring me baby Margaret to hold and snuggle. If it hadn't been for you, Margaret, I would have turned into a bitter unhappy woman."

"I didn't know that story."

"I know. But I'm telling you today for a reason. You saved me, and I love you as if you were my own daughter. I'll help you, but I don't want you to be put into a situation where you're in danger. God knows you have worked like a grown man since you were seven years old. I don't blame you for not wanting to go back home to the farm. Slave labour if you ask me. And going back to the convent? Well, that would be the day I'd ever send you back there. A load of crap sending you off to be a nun. I told your mother as much. But the day she married your father with that temper of his, and then turning Catholic for him, I knew there'd be big trouble down the road. Sweetie, I want you here with me more than anything in world. Always have. But you're better off getting away from this place cause, truthfully, I don't know what your father will do to you if he gets a hold of you. I would be fearful for your life if you stayed here. And I could not live with that."

"But what am I going to do then? And where can I go?"

"Let's think about a plan. Maybe head west to Calgary where I hear life is grand. My friend Gigi went there two years ago, and she loves it. I've been thinking about going there myself."

Aunt Beatrice had been talking about leaving Halifax ever since Margaret could remember. But she heard her mother once say that she didn't have the guts to leave Nova Scotia. Margaret didn't think that was true. If anyone didn't have guts it was her mother for never standing up for herself or her children against her abusive husband.

Beatrice called her parents the next morning to let them know she had left the convent. Her aunt explained to Margaret that the reason she was calling them was she wanted to get to them first before the convent got a hold of them.

"Just letting you know, Frankie. Margaret has left the convent and has come here. She doesn't want to go back."

Margaret held her ear to the telephone beside her aunt's ear so she could hear the conversation.

"What the hell you talkin' bout? She better get her arse back to the convent right this minute!"

"I'm telling you, Frankie; she is not going back there. I just wanted to let you know she's all right. I've got her here. There is nothing more to say."

"Mary, get over here and talk some sense into yur crazy sister," he screamed.

They waited till her mother got on the phone.

"You got no right to keep her, she has a destiny to be a nun, plain and simple," Margaret heard her mother say.

"I'm not taking her there, and that's that, Mary," Beatrice said. "You can scream at me all you want."

"The shame she is going to cause us. You just don't understand. I won't be able to show my face in church."

"Really? You would rather have this beautiful, talented hard-working girl be eternally unhappy just so you look good at your Catholic church? Please listen to yourself, dear sister!"

"You don't understand my life."

"You're right about that. I don't know how you married that man in the first place. Why you let him beat you and the children, I'll never know. Our parents taught us to be good Protestant Christians without shoving it down our throats. Then Frankie comes along and all of a sudden you believe Protestants are beneath you and that the Catholics are the only way to assure you go to heaven. Really? And then to sacrifice your daughter's happiness so you look good at church or somehow get extra points to get you into heaven? Frankie beats you and the children all the time. Well, I guess you need all the extra points you can get! Regardless, Mary, if Frankie shows up at my door, I'll call the police. Margaret will be here for another day, then she is heading out west, so I suggest you give that husband of yours some story to keep him off her trail. I only called because you're still my sister, and I don't want you to worry about her."

Margaret knew her aunt had gone too far. The silence on the other end of the phone was evidence that she had hit a nerve. She was sure that Greta, the telephone operator, was listening in as she always did on the party lines. She knew enough to know that the conversation would be the latest gossip.

Her aunt finally broke the silence and softly asked, "Do you want to talk to your daughter?"

The reply from her mother was slow and weak. "I can't."

Beatrice and Margaret talked all day about everything from "the birds and the bees" to how to apply for jobs, to the importance of proper English, and how to protect herself from men.

"Be sure not to make eye contact with them. Sit beside only women. Kick them between the legs if they try and touch you, and then run and scream for help. Never believe them because most of them lie and want only one thing."

Margaret smiled as her aunt went on with her advice, frantically trying to teach her everything she needed to know for the rest of her life. She was not afraid, not even of her father right now. She knew she could outrun any man who tried to touch her. She might be a little thinner than normal, but she hadn't lost her strong muscles; she was still as strong as an ox. Throwing bales, carrying pails and children, and shoveling grain for hours had kept her lean—there was not an ounce of fat on her. She was pure muscle even after three months of hardly eating at the convent. Most importantly though, was her attitude. She felt stronger than ever, and if she had to, she knew she had a rage deep inside her that she could let out, and it would scare even the most dangerous man.

Beatrice gave Margaret the three hundred dollars that she had been saving for when she decided to leave Nova Scotia, and she bought her some clothes, a suitcase, and a train ticket to Calgary. She sent a telegram to her friend Gigi, who had moved to Calgary two years prior, asking that she meet her niece at the train station and help her get settled.

"Margaret, you know you're a gifted girl. You're not only strong on the outside. You're strong on the inside. More than you even know. You can make a good life for yourself; I'm positive of that. You can work and get your grade twelve easily. All that homework I have given you since you left school, you excelled at it. You'll graduate in no time, then you can go on to become a teacher like me or do whatever job you want. But my advice is to get a good profession like teaching so that you'll always have work and be able to support yourself."

"I think I want to be a famous singer-songwriter."

"I know, sweetie, but it is not an easy career to get into, especially for women. And remember, it is important to not rely on any man for money. You need to get your own profession. Give teaching a thought. You're a natural."

"Yes, I see that, Auntie. I loved helping out the teachers with the small children in school, and I was always teaching my sisters stuff. I guess teaching is good, too, cuz I can have the summers off to travel and sing."

"Yes, there is that advantage. Only you can decide, Margaret. It is your life. You're so smart; I know you will figure it all out. The thing is, my advice, take it or leave it, is you need to have a true profession first, so you don't need to rely on any man for money. I know I keep saying that, but that's what I did when my husband walked out on me. I could have easily been living in poverty if I hadn't got myself a teaching certificate. Believe me, young lady, you have to take care of yourself first. The one good thing about your child-hood is that you learned early on what you don't want in life. Some of us take a lifetime to figure that out. Knowing what you don't want is as important as knowing what you do want."

Margaret thought long and hard about everything her aunt had said that night.

"How can my life of being beaten and unloved by my parents, leaving school in grade six, and working like a dog be a good thing?" she wondered.

One by one, she went through how those experiences were going to help her to survive in the future. When she came downstairs for breakfast the next morning, she had a smile on her face.

"Auntie, I get what you were trying to say yesterday. At first, I thought you were not making sense. But I get it now. I wrote down in my diary all the ways my life so far will help me. I worked like a dog, but when I think about it, I love working. I like the feeling of accomplishing something; creating meals is fun. I'm strong physically, and I'm proud of that. It is better than being a weakling. I love learning, and I love teaching! So, I know I'll be okay to get my grade twelve, and I would be a good teacher. I know I never want to hit children or put clothespins on their ears as punishment. And if I ever have children, which I doubt I ever will cuz I don't want to ever get married, I won't have too many. I'll love them, and hug them, and support their dreams like you have mine, and I'll always be there for them. I can still have my music career, too, if I'm a teacher. I can go to festivals in the summer and perform on weekends and holidays, and then one day when I get famous, I can quit teaching and do my music full-time. I get it, Auntie. You're so wise!"

Beatrice got up from her chair and hugged her niece. She took Margaret's face into her hands and gently kissed her forehead.

"Sweetie, I just know you're going to have a wonderful life." She grasped Margaret's hand and gently placed it on Margaret's own chest. "And remember, I'm here in your heart always."

"Thank you. I know you are. And I'll write to you every week, I promise."

"And I'll write to you! Now I know Gigi will help you get started in Calgary. She is one of my best friends, and she will be there for you when you arrive. She answered my last telegram, and she said she would love to help you and can't wait to meet you. I'll send her a telegram today to let her know when you will be getting there. Now let's get moving, time is a wasting!"

They stood on the station platform, silently holding hands as they looked earnestly for the train to come around the bend. Margaret was in her new, green flowered dress and matching hat, and she clutched her new suitcase and new guitar case that her aunt had bought her last Christmas.

When the train finally arrived, her aunt kissed her goodbye and gave her the longest hug she had ever had in her life.

"We will keep in touch. Every week we will write each other. And who knows, I may come to visit someday soon," she said, tears streaming down her face.

For the first time in her life, Margaret felt free to pursue her dreams. She felt no fear as she boarded the train. She had a plan, and she would stick to it no matter what.

Sarah, age six

"Mommy, look a train just like the one I was on!"

"We were never on a train, honey."

"Yes, when I was that girl. I went on a train all by myself. I even slept on the train. And I saw purple grass."

"Purple?"

"Where were you going on the train?"

"To Calgary."

1933 - Calgary

Dear Auntie,

Well, I arrived in Calgary! What an amazing train ride. I hardly slept because I didn't want to miss anything. My favourite was the prairies with the miles and miles of flat land, and the amazingly beautiful purple flax in bloom, and the wheat fields, and hay bales, and all the small towns.

Everyone on the train talked about how the rain finally came for the farmers. Even though the prices are still low, they seem hopeful. Maybe the drought is over. We can only hope.

I was met with only kindness by the staff on the train and everyone else I encountered. I helped a nice lady who was traveling from Winnipeg with her three small children, so that kept me busy the last stretch. She was headed to Calgary where her husband had gotten a job in the oil industry. Everyone talked about how Alberta is booming because they are discovering oil everywhere. In the fields, the oil wells look like giant chickens pecking the ground. It is the funniest thing. So much to learn!

I was greeted by your lovely friend Gigi at the train station, and she was so helpful. I'm staying with her now until I find a place of my own. She has places lined up for me to see and even some job interviews. I couldn't have asked for a better introduction to Calgary. She is so generous. I can't imagine what it would have been like to arrive and not have anyone to greet me and help me get settled. I have you to thank. You're my saviour!

Gigi sends her love and wanted me to tell you that she is moving to Edmonton in two months, as she just got a job with the government there. She said she will write you and tell you all about it. She seems very happy about it. I already know I'll miss her!

    Love, Margaret

"Can you waitress? Any experience?" asked Mr. Rosi in a thick Greek accent. He was the owner of Santorini Restaurant.

"Well, you can say I have experience. I'm the oldest of twelve, and I cooked, cleaned, and looked after my siblings most of my life. My aunt says, 'There is no moss growing under my feet,' if you know what I mean, sir."

"Ah ha. No moss, eh? Well, we get busy here, and the hours are long. We open at six in the morning and close at eight in the evening, Monday to Saturday. I expect you to be here six days a week and work the full day. I'll feed you all your meals for free. Think you can handle that?"

"Yes, oh, yes! You won't be disappointed in the least."

"All right then, you start tomorrow. And tie that long hair of yours up good and tight so it doesn't get in the customers' food," he said with a big toothy smile. Then he took her hand with a hardy shake and a chuckle.

Nicholas Rosi, or as everyone called him, Nicky the Greek, was a well-known entrepreneur in Calgary, and every business he owned "turned to gold," Gigi told her before she left the apartment that day. "He's a fair man, Margaret, and if you work for him, he'll treat you well. And he feeds his staff, and that in itself, is great. His food is out of this world. I eat there a lot."

Margaret couldn't believe her luck. Her first interview and she got the job on the spot. She walked down the street a block from Santorini's. To her amazement there was sign on a door: *Room for Rent—Female Only.* She knocked. A middle-aged woman answered the door, and in a thick German accent, she said, "Can I help you, young lady?"

She had a round face and thin brown hair. Her eyes nearly disappeared when she smiled. She was short and had a flowered apron on over a blue dress and thick stockings on her plump legs. Her shoes looked like they had seen better days. She reminded Margaret of her own grandmother.

"I've come about the room for rent. I just got a job down the street at Santorini's Restaurant."

"Oh, *mein Gott!* I just put that sign up an hour ago! Must be somebody up above looking after me to send a nice young woman so quickly! Come in. Now, where are you from? Your accent, it's one I've never heard before."

"I'm from Eastern Canada, Nova Scotia to be exact. I moved here to work and save up enough money to go to Normal School and become a teacher."

"You're a little young, no? To be on your own?"

"I'm sixteen, ma'am, but I'm very mature for my age, and I'm determined to work hard and make money so I can go to school."

"Well, good for you. I like a woman who tries to get a profession. Wish I had done such a thing. But that is another story! Come in, and I'll show you the room."

Margaret noticed the small table near the door with paper and pencils on it and the telephone that hung above it. The wide mahogany staircase led to the second floor. She followed the woman up the stairs, noticing how she hung on tight to the banister, waddling slowly. This was an older home that must have been grand at one time. And though it was dark and the rugs looked worn, it smelled fresh and looked very clean.

"The room is not fancy, but it is practical. This used to be a room and board house in its day but not anymore. There is a little electric double burner and sink in the room, so you can do your own cooking. I don't clean. It is up to you to look after yourself. I'm not in good enough shape for any of that nonsense. I have someone who cleans the hallway for me once a week, but I ask that you leave your shoes at the entrance and wear slippers in the house. There is furniture in the room as well linen and dishes and a nice feather tic I brought from Germany, so you will be plenty warm. You must do your own laundry. The bathroom is down the hall. You have to share it with Lillian. She is clean and quiet. Her husband died, and she was left with nothing, poor thing. She works at the laundromat down the street. Not an easy job," she said, shaking her head.

As Margaret entered the room, she was shocked at how small it was. There was a long cot—which thankfully looked to be the right size for her, a tiny sink, a counter with a cooktop, and a shelf with some dishes and a single pot and pan. There was a dresser with a mirror, one chair, and a tiny table. The large window looked down at the street below. She noticed the walls were clean and smelled like they had been freshly painted.

In the wide hall the stairs went down in grand fashion, and on the other side there were also rooms with doors.

"Are there other people renting here besides Lillian?" asked Margaret as she pointed to the other side.

"Yes, I have two older bachelors over there. One works at a confectionary down the street. I am sorry to say the other man does not work. He is a drinker, but a nice man, but when he ties one on, he gets a little loud. Usually, he starts singing Gaelic songs. He comes from the East like you, but he has a different accent. You might understand Gaelic, but I surely don't. Harmless though, wouldn't hurt a flea. I haven't the heart to kick him out. Somehow, he pays his rent every month, though I don't know where he gets his money from. None of my business anyhow."

"Well, I think I'll take it if that is okay with you, ma'am."

"No more ma'am. Call me Mrs. Schmidt. My husband is Karl. He is pretty much an invalid, had a couple of strokes in his forties, so I take care of him. He walks, but it takes him an hour to cross the room. Ya. He doesn't talk much, as the whole side of his face is paralyzed, but he always has a nice, crooked smile for everybody. Poor soul, he's been like that for almost twenty years now."

Margaret nodded. Her brow furrowed in concern. "My name is Margaret, Margaret McLean."

"I'm happy to have you, Margaret, and you can stay for free till you get your first pay check for rent. It will be nice to have some young blood in the house!"

With that, she took Margaret's hand and patted it with both of hers, then guided her into her kitchen.

"Karl, come meet our new renter, Margaret," she yelled.

Margaret watched Karl get up from his chair in slow motion and shuffle slowly towards them. He was a thin man with grey hair and glasses that stood crooked on his face. His wife was right, he had the sweetest smile—one corner up, and the other drooped down. Margaret was shocked at how long it took him to get from the living room to the kitchen.

"Karl, go to the freezer and get some nice sugar cookies to send back with Margaret to share with her friends."

As Karl shuffled along, Mrs. Schmidt whispered to Margaret, "It's good to keep him moving, or else he'd sit there all day long."

Mrs. Schmidt served her a strong black coffee and a slice of apple cake, which she called *kuchen.*

Margaret found the coffee very strong but didn't say a word. The kuchen was delicious, and Margaret made sure to ask her for the recipe. Margaret and Mrs. Schmidt sat for an hour and got to know each other. Margaret felt that everything was working out perfectly. She felt hope and real joy—something she hadn't felt in a long time. It was like everything was falling into place, like there was some master plan. Maybe there *was* someone looking down on her. Maybe Mrs. McDonald's husband or a long-gone relative was guiding her and looking out for her. When she left Mrs. Schmidt's house, she gazed at the puffs of white clouds in a sea of blue in the sky and saw a brilliant beam of sunlight shining through like a divine message just for her. She felt her body tingle with excitement. She knew she was on the right path. She closed her eyes in reverence and said: "Thank you!"

C. INGRID DERINGER

July 25, 1938

Dear Auntie,

How are you? I hope you got over that flu. You sounded so tired in your last letter. That is not like you.

I'm getting so tired too, but it's not from the flu. I think I'm just tired of wait-ressing six days a week and cleaning offices on Saturday nights and Sundays. But I know the end is near. You'll be happy to know that I have saved up enough money for two years of Normal School and for a second-hand car, if you can believe it. My boss Nicky was buying a new car, so he let me buy his old one for a really good price. I'm so lucky. He is the nicest man, and his wife is, too, although I don't get to see her that much because she is busy at home with their six children. The one hundred dollars you sent was such a lovely gift! It paid for my tuition and books with a little leftover to buy a new outfit for college. When I think back, it has been a long five years. I have just been working the whole time and saving money, and I have not had a lot of time for fun, or sadly, to practice my guitar or harmonica. I have written a few songs, though, that I think are quite good. The one nice thing about cleaning offices is that no one is around, and I can sing to my heart's content. One of the songs I wrote called Tales of a Waitress is really good. I sang it to Nicky and the gang at work, and they loved it! It is based on the stories the regulars have told me when I work at the lunch counter. Like old mister Brown who lost his leg in the first war and came home to find his wife was in love with his best friend. And then there is Harry and Sylvia, an elderly couple who come in everyday dressed in identical outfits. They look like twins, but they are husband and wife. Anyway, I think it is a good song. I'll enclose a copy of the lyrics. Let me know what you think.

I know you asked me if I was lonely, but Auntie, I must say, I have not been lonely in the least. I have been too busy for that, and besides, everyone at the restaurant and Mr. and Mrs. Schmidt make me feel like I have a little family. They are all really happy for me. I think Nicky and his wife and the staff have finally given up on finding me a husband. They are always trying to set me up with a nice Greek boy! But I keep telling them I'm not going to get married, and that I want to become a famous singer and a teacher. They tease me about my dreams all the time. Nicky says when I find the right boy I'll know, and he says it would be a shame for me to be single. I just give up and laugh. They don't know how determined I really am!

I'm so excited to finally start school and not to work! Only one month left. I'm going to see about a boarding house tomorrow. I have three places to see. Wish me luck! Thank you from the bottom of my heart, Auntie, for always being there for me.

Love, Margaret

August 5, 1938, at the age of twenty-one, Margaret knocked on the door of Lily's Boarding House, two blocks away from the Normal School in Calgary.

"Welcome, you must be Margaret. Come in, come in."

It was a three-story house and fairly new from what Margaret could make out. The school had recommended it highly, saying that if Lily accepted her, she was very lucky.

Lily looked to be no more than forty-five years old. She was almost as tall as Margaret, and she was thin and lanky. She had a square jaw, and pink painted lips, and a smile that showed all her teeth. Her light brown hair was cut into a bob. And she wore pants! That was something Margaret had never seen women wearing except in magazines. Margaret thought she looked like a movie star.

Margaret wore her new outfit that she had bought at the Army and Navy Store. The dress had a black velvet collar and was in a shade of green that matched her eyes. She wore new black shoes with heels and had braided her hair—so long now that the braids nearly touched the floor. She thought she looked good, until she saw Lily.

Lily guided Margaret into the dining room. A large wooden table with eight chairs was in the centre of the room. A beautiful, shiny upright piano sat in one corner, and a large buffet with a mahogany clock lined the wall. The curtains were striped gold and beige, and there were expensive looking vases and statues and fresh flowers adorning every surface, their floral scent permeating the room. The word that came to Margaret's mind was: elegant. Margaret suddenly felt self-conscious. She wished her new outfit was sophisticated instead of practical and in some other colour than the same green she always wore.

They sat on a beautiful Victorian couch under the large picture window and sipped tea as Lily went over the rules and regulations of her boarding house.

"Supper is served at six o'clock sharp every weekday, and breakfast is served at eight. If you miss supper, you're free to go into the kitchen and eat your food cold. Weekends you're on your own. If you want to cook, you have to sign up on the chalkboard in the hall to use the kitchen. There is a fridge in the hall for your own food. Curfew is ten o'clock on weekdays, eleven on weekends. No boys in your room. I'm not your parent. You're an adult, and I trust my boarders keep to the rules. Rent is due the first of the month. I don't clean your room, but I'll give you clean linens and towels once a week. I clean the bathrooms every two days. You share the bathroom with three other girls on your floor. The boys are on the top floor. The dining room and living area are shared by all of you. Ed, my husband, is an engineer, and he works downtown. We have living quarters in the back behind that door. If you have an emergency just knock. Understood? Do you think you can stick by those rules, Margaret?"

"Yes, Mrs. Brooks, I don't have any problems with them at all. The rules seem reasonable, and I love the fact that I can do a little cooking. I love to cook, but the last five years I have had only a tiny electric burner in my room, so I have missed cooking terribly."

"Now tell me a little about yourself, Margaret." She placed her hand on Margaret's. It felt warm and soft. Margaret proceeded to tell Lily about her life in the last five years. She omitted any talk about Nova Scotia, except to say she had moved from there years ago. Margaret had decided the minute her feet hit Alberta soil that she would never reveal what her childhood was like to anyone. The past was over, and she wanted to keep it that way.

"May I say, Margaret, you sound like you have worked hard to get to where you are. I admire that in a woman. I think we will get along just fine. And please, from now on, call me Lily."

And with that, Margaret began her two-year stay at Lily's Boarding House.

On Margaret's first night at the boarding house, dinner was roast beef that melted in her mouth, mashed potatoes sprinkled with fresh dill, and peas—picked that morning from the garden—swimming in a light cream sauce with what Margaret thought was paprika sprinkled on top. The pepper gravy was the best gravy Margaret had ever tasted. For dessert, Lily made rhubarb-strawberry pie with a beautiful flaky crust that was crisscrossed on top and sprinkled with sugar.

During the meal Margaret closed her eyes to savour each bite, not realizing that the rest of them watched and listened as she grinned and let out little moans. One young man in particular couldn't keep his eyes off her. She was in a meditative state till the last bite, and then her thoughts went to the last home cooked meal that had tasted that good—over five years ago on her sixteenth birthday, the day before she left for the convent. She loved Nicky's Greek food, but somehow Lily's food was so comforting.

There were eight tenants, all students from the Provincial Trades and Arts Institute; four women from the Normal School Program, and four men from the Mechanics Program. She felt like she had made seven friends that first evening. They sat together at the table after the meal and talked till ten o'clock.

As they were putting their dishes in the kitchen and cleaning up, Rene, the young man from Prince Edward Island who was in the Farm Mechanics program, raced to stand beside her. She could feel his presence, and she turned and looked at him. She smiled, waiting for him to say something. She could see he was thinking of what to say. She waited. He looked at her for what seemed like eternity, his eyes darting from side to side. She could tell he was struggling.

"Is there something you want to say, Rene?"

"Margaret, would you like to go for a walk after classes tomorrow?" he blurted out as his face turned red.

"I would love to Rene."

His shoulders relaxed and a huge smile crossed his face, showing his dimples and his straight white teeth.

"Oh my gosh, he is so cute with his little French accent and that dark brown hair," she thought.

When he smiled, which he did most of the evening, his hazel eyes along with his bushy eyebrows turned way up. It was almost like he was asking: "Am I not the cutest thing you ever saw?" His cuteness made up for the fact that he was short. He was only five foot five she guessed, which normally would have been a deal breaker.

She couldn't stop smiling as she lay in her beautiful bed that evening. Her head swirled with thoughts of Rene, school, Lily, the meal, her new friends, and the beautiful linen sheets caressing her skin. It seemed to take forever to fall asleep. Never had she felt so happy, she decided as she closed her eyes.

"Why did you leave PEI?" she asked Rene.

"There was no work there anymore, and my papa wanted me to become a mechanic. He heard about Alberta and the Institute in Calgary and suggested I come and give it a try. He's a potato farmer, and he instilled in me from the time I was a kid that he wanted more for me. 'You're a natural mechanic, Rene,' he would say. 'Get a trade. Don't waste your time being a potato famer like me.' So, I came."

"Do you miss home?"

"Like the dickens! I miss my younger brother, Philip, and my parents, and the kitchen parties we had every weekend. How 'bout you?"

"Yes, well, coming from a Catholic family of twelve children living on a dairy farm and me being the oldest, I have to say I do miss some aspects of it, I guess, except for all the work or going to church and praying all the time. I was really fed up with the religious part by the time I left home. It is one of the reasons I don't go to church anymore."

"I was brought up Anglican, but we mostly just went to church at Christmas."

She couldn't believe she had broken her rule already about talking about home. But it just came out so quickly. She had let down her guard for a few minutes. Was it because he was so easy to talk to? Wanting to change the subject, she asked, "So you said you missed the kitchen parties in PEI. Is that like the Ceilidhs in Nova Scotia?"

"Yes, but just in peoples' homes. We have Ceilidhs, too, and they are more open to the public and usually held in the church basement or town hall like in Nova Scotia, I would guess. I like them all. I like any kind of music where you get together and sing, play music, and dance."

"I like the idea of a kitchen party. We should plan for one at the house. I wonder if Lily would mind? I never went to many Ceilidhs when I was growing up, but when my aunt took me, they were so much fun. Do you play an instrument?" she asked.

"I play guitar a little—not overly talented I'm afraid. My brother plays the fiddle, and he is pretty good, and my mama plays the banjo, and my papa the spoons! We are all quite amateur, but we enjoy it."

Margaret and Rene met every day after classes were out and walked home together. On the third week of doing this, Rene gently slipped his hand into hers as they walked.

She smiled at him, trying to look calm, but when their hands touched, electricity coursed throughout her body—a feeling she had never experienced in her life. She wondered if he felt the same thing, but she just stared ahead, afraid to look at him. It was strange, but she almost felt terrified, like she might raise off the ground and fly if she looked him in the eyes.

After the fourth week as he said goodnight to her on the stairs, he stepped up one step so that he was looking directly into her eyes. He put one hand on the wall behind her and leaned in, slowly and gently touching his lips to hers.

The kiss sent tingling sensations through them both. Margaret imagined that if someone were watching nearby, they may have seen sparkling-coloured lights circling their bodies from head to toe.

Dear Auntie,

I met a man! A nice one. In fact, he is too nice! He is so funny, and he makes me laugh like you wouldn't believe. His name is Rene, and he is an Acadian from PEI. He is living at the same boarding house I'm in. We clicked the moment we met. It was as if I knew him all my life. I feel so comfortable around him. It is so strange. And the great thing is, he doesn't have a mean bone in his body from what I can tell. I really like him! I just met him two months ago. It sounds so silly as I write this, but Auntie, all I can think about is him, day and night. Of course, not to worry, I'm still studying, and school is going fine. I find it easy and interesting, but I find my mind drifting off, thinking about Rene every five minutes! I can't wait for you to meet him. I apologize for not writing sooner about him, but I wanted to make sure it wasn't just an infatuation before I told you about him. I know you will like him right away. I have been on dates before, of course, with Greek boys that Nicky set me up with in the last five years, but I just didn't click with any of them, and I always stopped it before it got too far. In fact, I think I didn't have any more than two dates with any one man. But Rene, he is so different from any of the others I dated. So different! We have the same love of music, and he is also a hard worker. He's not real ambitious. He wants to be a farm mechanic which is a good profession. But somehow, he seems to fulfil something in me that I didn't realize I was missing. I know it sounds so crazy. And he is the cutest thing you ever saw.

We are thinking of starting a weekly kitchen party at the boarding house with Lily and Ed's permission, of course. Rene and I have worked out a plan and will talk to them this evening. We want to teach everyone East Coast songs to start with. I don't remember ever being so happy or having so much fun. I hope you come soon so you can meet everyone here.

Love with all my heart, Margaret

Before the second month was over, they had their first Friday Night Kitchen Party. It turned out that Isabelle, one of her roommates, could play piano by ear, and one of the boys was a fiddler, and Mr. Brooks had been playing the banjo by himself for three years and thought it was a great opportunity for him to learn how to play with other people. The Friday Night Kitchen Party became a tradition at Lily's Boarding House for the next two years.

On the one-year anniversary of Margaret's stay at Lily's Boarding House, everyone gathered at the supper table including Lily and Ed. They were all eager to share stories of their month off. Most of the tenants had been gone the entire time visiting family, but Rene and Margaret had stayed and explored Calgary and the mountains and the lakes nearby. She was excited to introduce him to her adopted family—The Santorini's Restaurant gang and Mr. and Mrs. Schmidt.

Margaret stood up and made a toast before the meal started.

"You're all about to be treated to a Greek meal prepared by Chef Rene this evening. As you all know, I waitressed at the famous Santorini Restaurant before going to college. Now the owner, Nicky Rosi known as *Nicky the Greek,* makes the best authentic Greek food in the city. I worked there for five years, and I never heard of him sharing a recipe ever. It was a running joke that if Nicky died, Santorini's would have to change its entire menu. He personally made all his sauces fresh every day. Well, that all changed when I took Rene to meet the gang at the restaurant and we ate a meal there. Now I quote Rene verbatim:

"Nicky, if you don't teach me how to cook this food, I don't know how I can go on living. I mean this has got to be the best food I have ever eaten in my entire life! Now I grew up with meat and potatoes, lots of home-grown vegetables, and a little French cooking from what my mother remembered, but she was an orphan, Nicky, and well, let's just say there was no love in her cooking. This, Nicky, is love. You can feel the love you put into this food. You can taste the love."

Everyone at the table laughed.

"Needless to say, by the time we left the restaurant, Nicky and Rene had plans to meet on Sunday morning for Rene's first cooking class. In exchange, Rene would work on Nicky's wife's car. So folks, you're about to taste Rene's first Greek meal, and for your information, all the ingredients are courtesy of Nicky the Greek, who imports them directly from Greece. Enjoy!"

"To Chef Rene!" she said.

They all clapped and cheered.

Lily and Margaret served the dolmades, and olives, and zucchini fritters with tarragon and garlic sauce, then a glass of Retsina served with Greek salad, shish kebabs and keftedes— which Rene explained were meatballs cooked with herbs and onions—as well as roast potatoes with rosemary. To end the meal, Rene served piping hot espresso coffee with ouzo and whipped cream in the smallest teacups Lily had.

"In Greece," Rene explained, "they drink espresso, which is really strong coffee, out of tiny cups. The ouzo is a liquor which tastes a lot like licorice. Nicky said normally it is just the ouzo and espresso, but he likes to add fresh whipped cream on top for special occasions."

They all took a sip, and Rene smiled at the sounds of satisfaction.

"I can see that Margaret's delight with food has rubbed off on all of you!"

They all laughed.

"The dessert, "Rene further explained, "is baklava. I made it from scratch, and I'll be honest with you, it is not as good as Nicky's, and I'm not sure why. It tastes good, but I think his is sweeter. I'll have to save him a piece and ask him where I went wrong. Anyway, let me know what you think."

There were more sounds of pleasure as they tasted the delicious dessert, and many of them closed their eyes while they ate. Margaret smiled to herself; they did all sound like her! Everyone said the meal was beyond delicious, and at the end they applauded, and Rene stood up and took a huge bow, grinning from ear to ear.

Lily took pictures of all the food, and later she gave copies to Nicky who proudly framed them and hung them in his office, and they made him smile every time he looked at them.

Margaret had never seen him cooking in the kitchen. She was always the one to make Sunday meals, often for the whole house, especially when she could get fresh produce from the market. Everyone in the house knew she loved to cook, and they were happy to pitch in for groceries if she cooked the meals on the weekends. But never once had she heard from Rene that he liked to cook. She smiled to herself.

As if reading her mind, Lily said, "Nothing sexier than a man who can cook, and that was one fine meal." She winked at Margaret.

Margaret blushed.

That night as she lay in bed, she thought about the last month of their time together. They had fished on the Bow River with a picnic lunch under the shade, walked trails in the foothills, danced in the moonlight in front of Lake Louise, and soaked in the hot springs in Banff. She remembered telling her aunt that she had wanted to see the world and travel, and this last month was like her dream came true. There was so much to see and explore, and they only had to drive a few hours away from home. It was the most amazing area. They saw the prairies, the foothills, the majestic mountains, and ice-fed lakes that were emerald green, all within a day's drive from Calgary.

When they went to visit Mr. and Mrs. Schmidt, Rene had Mr. Schmidt in tears from laughing so hard telling him jokes and doing impersonations of his family back home. She realized that she had known Mr. Schmidt for six years and in that time, she had seen him slow down even more. The strokes that had robbed him of so much were taking their toll. His shuffle was minute now, just one tiny step and a weak drag of his left leg. It was sad to see him deteriorating. She had never seen him laugh out loud the whole time she knew him. He smiled his crooked smile enough, but she never saw him actually laugh till Rene came to visit. As Mrs. Schmidt was seeing them to the door, she told Rene, "You have made my husband a very happy man today. I haven't seen him laugh like that in many, many years. Thank you." And she patted his shoulder. Then she looked at Margaret and said, "You found a good man, my dear. A good man." And Margaret smiled.

"I know."

Then she remembered the visit to Santorini's when Rene made his deal with Nicky to exchange cooking classes for mechanic work. She looked at him and said, "Who are you, where did you come from, and where did you learn to sweet talk like that?" To which he just laughed.

It suddenly occurred to her that ever since she had met Rene, whenever they walked down the street, people always smiled at them. Up until the day she saw him in action with Nicky the Greek, she had thought it was because she was six foot one and he was five foot five and people probably thought they were an odd-looking couple. She wasn't sure how she hadn't noticed it before, but as Rene walked, he tipped his hat and smiled at every single person. "No wonder people look at us," she thought, "it isn't that we are an odd-looking couple, it is because Rene is a "ham" as Aunt Bea would say, and he can charm the pants off anyone."

As Margaret thought about the two of them together, her heart swelled. Rene was the kind of person everyone loved. He gained more friends in one year than she had in six years of living in Calgary. As they walked to school, she was always amazed at how many people he said hello to and how many he knew by name, from the baker, to the mailman, to the children in the street, to neighbours, and to people from every program at the college. It was really quite astonishing when she thought about it.

Dear Auntie,

I hope you're well and not working too hard harvesting your garden. It sounds like you had a heck of a nice crop. I miss having a garden. One day! I only have one year left. Can you believe it? This year went by so fast. I really enjoy school and find it super easy. Next year we begin to go to actual classrooms to observe, and then do a few lessons with the children. I hope they send me to a place in Calgary so I don't have to leave Lily's Boarding House. I love it here! Especially after this last summer break from school. Rene and I had the most wonderful month. We went to see the hot springs; we danced in the moonlight at Lake Louise; we hiked the mountains; and we swam in the ice-cold lakes near Banff. There is so much to see and do here. I have lived in Calgary for six years, but until this break, the only place I ever ventured to was Millarville to the market on the weekends in the summer and fall!

Rene planned most of our outings, and he would leave me little clues on love notes of where we were going next. He is so romantic! I'm beginning to feel that life without Rene would be utterly boring. We laugh so much it is as if I'm making up for all the anger and tears from my childhood. He is like a gift from the universe that has wiped out all the bad. Does that sound too strange?

I'm sorry, I know I go on and on about Rene all the time. But if you met him, or when you meet him, you will see why.

All my love, Margaret

P.S. Can you send me your mustard recipe? Mother's mustard is good, but yours is better. I want to know your secret. Lily and I are planning to make mustard and relish together.

"Miss Margaret McLean, your assignment is a one room schoolhouse in Black Diamond, please come get your information package."

Margaret's heart sank. Two months away from Rene and all her friends at the boarding house was not what she was hoping for. She had really wanted to get a school in Calgary.

She opened the package and read: *Your billet is with the Wagner family. They own the local hotel. You will be staying in a guest room with a sink and toilet. A bathtub is down the hall and shared with other hotel guests.*

It looked quite modern and clean from the pictures. "Well, at least I'll have some privacy," she thought. As she read on, she was surprised that she only stayed Monday to Thursday at her billet. Fridays she had to be back at the college.

"I won't miss our kitchen parties!" she said out loud.

Everyone in the class looked up, and the laughter startled her. She smiled. The class was used to Margaret's habit of talking aloud to herself.

"Yes, Margaret, you're all in your new schools for four days, and then back here on Fridays. Now when you get to your schools, be on your best behaviour. Many of you have posts in communities that are growing, and they are looking for teachers, and so it may land you a job as soon as you graduate. Fridays we will debrief here and talk about your experiences and observations in the classrooms. This will be the time to ask questions and bring up any concerns you have. Take notes so you're prepared each Friday to report on your week. Any questions? Good, class dismissed, have a great weekend," said Professor Jenkins as he waved his hand in the air.

As Margaret walked home, she remembered what Aunt Beatrice told her in her last letter. "If you do get an out-of-town billet, it is not always a bad thing for relationships. Lord Byron, the poet, whom I'm reading right now, says, 'Absence—that common cure of love.' If it is love, sweetie, then it will grow even more when you're apart."

Her aunt was so wise. If she and Rene were truly meant to be together, this time apart would be a good test.

The year went by quickly, and her time away in Black Diamond was good for her. She focused on her teaching instead of wholly on Rene. She loved the Wagner family, and they were very respectful of her privacy. She felt inspired by the warm people and the beautiful foothills, and she wrote three songs. One in particular, about sweet, inquisitive Frances Wagner, who was one of her grade two students, was especially good. Her parents kept asking her if it was okay that Frances would come upstairs and visit her or walk with her to school every day.

"Please let us know if our little Frances is bothering you. She talks about you constantly. She is a handful," Mrs. Wagner said.

"I don't mind one bit. She is extremely bright and inquisitive, and I find her very entertaining!" Margaret said, and it was the truth.

She never got tired of her questions.

Why Miss McLean, do we have belly buttons? I really don't see a purpose for them? What is the biggest bird in the world, Miss McLean? Why do we have two eyes if we only see one thing? If plants need rain and sun to grow, and rainbows are made of light and water, are rainbows like plant food? What did it feel like the last day you were a child?

Margaret was used to children, having eleven younger siblings, but this little Frances was nothing like any of them.

"I must stay in touch with this girl and see what she does with this incredible, insatiable appetite for knowledge. She will do something extraordinary I'm sure," she thought.

The last four months of college, Margaret applied for teaching positions and began to think about what her future would look like. She didn't want to give up on her dream. She had pictured herself on stage performing since she was six years old. But how she would ever achieve that, she wasn't sure. She knew her aunt was right, having a teaching career was at least a solid profession that gave her freedom in so many ways. She didn't have to rely on anyone else, she could save up money to buy anything she wanted, and best of all, she could always do her singing on the weekends and summers off. It was the best plan, but she could see that it was getting more complicated. And then there was the issue of figuring out how, or if, Rene fit into her plans.

1940-1944

It was a hot spring day in 1940, and twenty-three-year-old Margaret McLean was heading out the door of Lily's Boarding House. Just as she placed her hand on the front doorknob, Rene came flying down the stairs.

"Wait, Margaret. I have something for you."

"Oh, goodness. You startled me. What is it? I'm just heading out to the Millarville Market to pick up some fresh vegetables and a chicken for supper. I'll be back soon."

He handed her a small, light brown leather case.

"Rene, what in the world. What is it? A harmonica?"

"Well, I know the one you got from your dad is not that great, and I think you deserve a really good one."

"But it isn't my birthday or our anniversary. Why are you buying me a gift?"

"It is just a little something special. Enjoy!" he said with a huge smile. He turned and ran back up the stairs.

"He seems so excited," Margaret thought, "like a little kid in a candy shop."

"Well, thank you!" she yelled, and she put the harmonica in her purse.

She rolled down the window of her black, 1938 Chevrolet as soon as she was out of the city limits, then breathed deeply, allowing the smell of freshly cut hay to fill her whole body. She let out a long drawn out "ahh." It was one of her favourite smells. She watched as the prairie turned into gentle, rolling hills. She smiled at the picture-perfect snow-topped majestic Rocky

Mountains in the distance, a backdrop to the fields dotted with square hay bales and cows grazing in the fields.

She always felt a sense of peace and calm come over her when she left the city and headed to Millarville, but today she felt a hint of anxiety as she glanced over at the harmonica sticking out of her purse.

"Damn you, Rene! What are you up to?"

She had been coming to the market for three years. Nicky had told her years ago that it was a great place to get fresh meat and vegetables direct from the farmers. When she bought her car, it was her first trip out of the city, and ever since then she had been hooked on Millarville. It wasn't just the market, it was the drive into the country, the scenery, the smells, and the people.

Perhaps a part of her missed the farm in Nova Scotia where she grew up and that was what drew her. But she would never admit that to anyone—not even herself.

She grabbed her basket and made her way to the vegetable stands.

"Ahh, fresh potatoes, I'll take five pounds of the red ones, please," she said, envisioning her plan for fried oregano chicken, roasted potatoes with fresh parsley and sour cream to dabble on top, and slightly cooked green beans with minced garlic marinated in salt and then added to olive oil as a dressing.

"We should have carrots by next week, Margaret," said Charles.

"Are your chickens ready yet?"

"No, a couple of more weeks, but Harry just did his butchering yesterday, so you should be able to get some from him."

"Thanks, Charles, and do say hi to Freida for me, and tell her I can't wait to see the new baby!"

"Will do, Margaret, see you next week, enjoy your day," he said as he handed her the bag of new, red baby potatoes.

As she walked to the next table, she heard Charles say to his brother, "Such a nice young woman and beautiful, too. Can't miss her in a crowd with that flaming red hair, braided and reaching almost to the ground, and those bright green eyes. My, she is tall for a woman, isn't she? Must be over six feet for sure. Shame she is not married. She would make a fine wife."

Margaret smiled to herself. It wasn't the first time she had heard such talk. It was like a recurring theme—comments about her looks and the fact that she was single and not married yet.

It was hot out, and there was not a cloud in the sky nor a breath of wind. As she walked to her car, she wondered about the harmonica in her purse. She wasn't ready to go back to the city yet. Often times when she finished shopping, she would go for a walk in the country. She was drawn to dusty country roads. It was so quiet, just the sound of her shoes crunching on the gravel, bugs buzzing, and sometimes grasshoppers flinging themselves in the air and the sound of them landing with a click.

She drove a few minutes, searching for a dirt road that looked deserted. When she finally found one north of the market, she took the harmonica out of her purse and opened the leather case. She looked to see if anyone was around. Not a soul.

She got out of the car and looked around again. When she was sure no one was around, she placed the harmonica to her lips and gently blew in and out, trying to find where the notes were and how to get a good clear sound. The sound was so rich and pure compared to the harmonica she had that had been her father's. And it was easy to play and felt so natural, as if it was just an extension of her voice. Within a few minutes she was so immersed in her playing, and concentrating so hard on figuring out how to play her new song "Taking a Train to Anywhere but Home," that she wasn't worried if anyone saw or heard her or not. She walked along the dirt road for over an hour, playing the harmonica and singing. When she finally quit playing, contentment washed over her, and if you were to look very closely, you would have noticed a slight flutter of her heart underneath her baby-blue sun dress.

"Is this Rene's way of showing me that he supports my dream of a music career?" she asked herself as she slipped the harmonica back into its case.

Out of the corner of her eye, she noticed something strange. What was that? She pulled the harmonica out of its case again, and there it was: an inscription on the back that she hadn't noticed before. It read: *Will you marry me?*

"Holy Liftin Dina! Would you look at that!" she said out loud to no one.

She sat in her car and stared at the pasture in front of her. She knew deep down it was coming. After two years together, she could read him like a book. But still, she was stunned. She had no plans whatsoever to get married to anyone, ever. She had made a vow to herself at sixteen that she was going to have a career in music, and a husband and children would spoil her plans. Not only that, she had seen how marriage changed men. Look at her father. Her mother had said he was so nice when he was courting her, but then he turned into a controlling, mean, angry, abusive man. And look at sweet Aunt Beatrice. She married her best friend, but after one year of marriage he walked out on her, and she never heard from him again.

But Rene was different, she was sure of that. He was everything that any woman could ever want in a man. And he was nothing like her father and seemed nothing like Aunt Beatrice's husband, although to be truthful, Margaret had never met the man because she was a baby when he walked out on her aunt. But still, to walk out without a word?

Neither was Rene anything like the few men she had dated over the years who were just so boring. He brought so much joy, laughter, adventure, and yes, music into her life in the last two years. He was so full of life. And he *did* seem to get who she was, and he knew about her hopes and dreams of making it in the music industry.

"The harmonica was proof of that—wasn't it?" But he was not perfect. She talked out loud to herself as she often did. "He's silly and fun, but he also naïve, or dare I say, simple."

She sat in her car, going over and over it all in her mind, dissecting Rene's personality, asking herself questions, and then answering herself. Rambling on and on.

"Do I really want to be with someone whose life ambition is to have fun? It seems to me that life for him is all about joking around, telling stories, and wanting to always have everyone around to party with. The only ambition I've heard him talk about is being a farm mechanic. Nothing wrong with being a mechanic; it is a very good vocation. He is a good worker, though, always helping Lily with repairs at the boarding house or helping the neighbors paint their houses, and he's always out cutting people's lawns. He is not lazy, and that is important. I could never stand for someone who was lazy. He doesn't have a mean bone in his body that I can see, and that is super important. He is the exact opposite of Father. Now that in itself, is reason enough to marry the man! And really—life without Rene just doesn't even seem like an option. Do I love him? That is the real question, isn't it? If someone asked me right here and now if I love Rene, without hesitation the answer would be 'yes.' But maybe I should hesitate. Just because you love someone you don't have to marry them and spend the rest of your life with them, even though that is what society seems to dictate. Aunt Beatrice taught me differently— that you don't have to marry to be happy. The question becomes: can I have a life with him and still follow my dreams? If I knew for sure, I wouldn't be having this conversation with myself now, would I? My goodness, I feel like a dog chasing its tail."

After an hour of contemplating and going around in circles, she decided to close her eyes, and then, like Aunt Beatrice had taught her so long ago, she tuned into her Margaret seed in the middle of her chest.

She heard her aunt's words in her head. "Close your eyes and find your "Margaret seed" that lives inside you. Ask it what it truly wants."

She closed her eyes and took long slow breaths till she felt her body begin to let go. She then brought her attention to the middle of her chest. She watched her breath go in and out through her nose and noticed how her chest rose up and down and up and down with each breath. When she felt totally relaxed, she simply asked, "What do I want? What do I really, really want?" And then it came to her, not gently but with a force. "Marry him, Margaret, for heaven's sake!"

Startled, she opened her eyes. "Wow!"

But no sooner was "Wow," out of her mouth when she heard a loud, clear voice inside her head. "Don't do it! You made a vow you would never marry because no man, no matter who he is, will ever support you having a career in music. You know if you marry him, you will have to at least put your music on hold. Can you live with that?"

On a warm, sunny day in August 1940, at the age of twenty-three, Margaret married Rene at City Hall in Calgary. Standing up for them was Aunt Beatrice and Rene's younger brother Philip, who had followed his brother to Calgary. He was living at Lily's Boarding House and had enrolled in Normal School. It was a small, intimate group that witnessed their vows: their roommates, Lily and Ed Brooks, the Schmidt's, Nicky and his wife, and Rene's parents. That evening, if you happened to be looking in the big picture window at the front of Lily's Boarding House, you would have seen a tall, thin, beautiful woman dressed in a simple, but elegant off-white dress, her long, wavy red hair braided with daisies and nearly touching the floor. You would have seen her dancing with a handsome, short, dark-haired young man in a tweed vest with matching pants and a crisp white shirt. Even if you lived down the block, you would have heard music playing and singing and laughter till the wee hours of the night.

Dear Auntie,

You probably aren't even home yet from your train trip as I write this. But I just had to tell you right away. You know the market I took you to in Millarville when you were here? Well, as you know, the little town was my secret escape when I first got my car. I had even applied to work at the school there. I never thought I would get it, though. I thought I would end up in the city. Not that I don't like the city, but when I go to Millarville, I don't know, I just feel so free, and calm, and welcomed. You can't get that feeling in a city. Anyway, I got the job! I start in September! The school is called Sheep Creek School, and I have grades one to twelve. I just had to write and let you know.

And by the way, thank you again for the sourdough starter! What a gift! I still can't believe you traveled on a train three-quarters of the way across Canada with it. But I guess with the stories you told me—about how the sourdough starter came from Ireland with Grandmother on a boat—makes a trip across Canada seem like nothing! I never knew you could dry the starter and store it, which led me to do a little research. Well, Lily and I brought it back to life, and we made our first sourdough bread. Everyone loved it! It was the first time I had sourdough since leaving home. It is one thing I really missed when I moved here. What a feeling to know that each loaf has some molecules from the old country or maybe even Egyptian times! Crazy when you think about it. Anyway, it was an amazing gift, and I'll make sure to share it! Maybe I'll even share it with my own children one day! You're the best!

Love, Margaret

P.S. Rene just informed me that he got a job apprenticing as a mechanic in Millarville. Can you believe it!? The universe is looking after us once again!

Dear Margaret,

I just got home and found your letter waiting for me. I'm so happy for you! Millarville is such a lovely little town. I loved my visit there and instantly saw why you fell in love with the area. I still have vivid pictures in my mind of the amazing scenery, and I shall treasure the memories of all the trips we made to the mountains and lakes and just driving in the foothills. Even though I enjoyed Calgary, I can totally see how beautifully you and Rene will fit into your little town.

Speaking of Rene, even though I know I told you I loved him, I want you to know that I really, really love him! He is a gem! All your hand-picked "family," too. They are all such genuine people, and I see how they adore you to pieces. I'm so very proud of you and so happy for you! I realized once I got home that I know one day I'll move out west to live near you. After seeing you, I realized how much I miss you being in my life— in person that is! I miss all our long talks.

I must tell you about my little side adventure on the way back to Halifax. I got off the train in Toronto. I had heard so much about it, and so I thought I would just spend a few days looking around. I also have to admit something to you that was in the back of my mind. I had heard through the grapevine many years ago that my husband George had moved there and was working as an actor in a theatre. I told myself that if I saw him, I would ask for a proper divorce. I had little information to go on, but I went downtown and walked and looked at theatres. After asking around, I tracked him down within one day. The theatre community I gather, is small. My heart was racing so fast that I thought my heart would come out of my mouth when I knocked on the door of his dressing room. He was as handsome as ever, and my heart sank. He was in shock when he saw me, to say the least! We met after his show for a drink and a meal. By the way, he was magnificent—which I knew he would be. He was always chosen for the leading roles in the school productions. I mean he could dance, sing, and act. Performing was in his blood! I was so surprised to find that his partner was a man. I thought it was odd that he said partner but I soon realized he is a homosexual. He came right out and told me. His partner Jack is an architect and is so sweet. You can see the love they have for each other just as plain as day. At first, I thought, God I wish he would have told me before. It would have saved me all the pain and shame I went through when he left. But I realized that life is not like that. As I remember telling you, I learned so much from that experience, and I grew in so many ways because of it. I became a teacher. I learned so much from healing myself from the depression I experienced. I learned so much I could fill a book!

The three of us spent the day together in Toronto. They showed me the sights and even drove me to the train station the next day. George said he would gladly sign the divorce papers. He begged me to forgive him over and over, and of course, I told him I did and that knowing why he left was the only thing holding me back all these years.

It all seems a dream now that I'm home. But I feel a sense of peace that I haven't felt in over twenty-two years! There was always a feeling that I was missing a piece to the puzzle, if that makes any sense. I have to admit that the one thing I was still hanging onto after all this time was a lack of trust in men. And I think I might have tried to push that onto you. But meeting Rene, I see my push didn't stick. Thank goodness. Rene is not someone you want to let go of. Anyway, back to my story, which I know I didn't share with you before as, to be honest, I was too embarrassed.

George and I were best friends growing up, inseparable since we were babies. We were next door neighbours, and I don't ever remember a time we were not together, from the sandbox to our high school graduation. Our mothers would laugh that we were like twins, finishing each other's sentences. When we graduated it just seemed that the natural thing to do was get married. I never knew anything about homosexuality in those days, and I still don't know much about it now. It just was not on my radar. Of course, looking back now, I can see the signs! We were more best friends than lovers. I like to think that if he would just have told me the truth, I would have accepted it, and we could have dealt with our break-up in a mature and loving way, but life is not like that. We can't go back, and to be truthful, I really have no idea how I would have reacted. No one ever knows. We tell ourselves stories about the past and the future, and really, the only thing that we can be certain of is right this minute, right now! So, what I know right now is that I feel so calm and happy. I have been blessed. This whole trip was all about seeing and feeling so much love. I feel like I'm swimming in an ocean of love! Thank you, dear Margaret.

I send you a giant wave of love, Aunt Beatrice.

Margaret read the letter over twice. After all these years she saw how her aunt lived with the shame and guilt of having been abandoned by her husband. It explained so much: why she never dated, and why she seemed not to trust men in general. And then added to that her brother-in-law whom she watched erode her sister's spirit and turn her into his workhorse and baby-making punching bag.

"Was she influenced by her aunt's beliefs?" she wondered. Is that why she struggled so much with the idea of marrying Rene? Thinking about it made her realize that throwing all men into a category was silly. Rene was so opposite her father, and of George, too. As soon as they were married, she could see that she had made the right decision. Would the marriage affect her dreams and hopes? There was no way of knowing really. But she was sure the harmonica was a good indication that he was going to be supportive of her plans for a music career.

Dear Auntie,

Wow! Your last letter was a real shocker. Thank you so much for sharing your news. I'm so happy that you have finally resolved the painful mystery that must have plagued you. I, too, do not know much about homosexuality, but I can imagine that it must be difficult to openly admit to being one. On the one hand, I can see that George must have struggled immensely; on the other hand, I do so wish he could have told you so you did not have to suffer so much. But I have to say, as you have taught me only too well, that we must make the best out of a bad situation. And you excelled at that. Look at all you have accomplished, and if all this wouldn't have happened, I would never have had you as my saviour. I owe you my life when I think of it. I can't even begin to imagine what would have happened to me if I had not had you in my life. So next time you see George, give him a hug from me and say thank you. Sounds strange, but life is strange, isn't it?

I wish you were still here, as I would give you one of the famous giant hugs that a certain person taught me when I was a little girl.

I love you with all my heart,

Margaret.

On the morning of their sixth-month anniversary, the sun rose as they made love in their tiny rental house on the edge of town. The crowing rooster next door was drowned out by Rene and Margaret's giggles.

"How did your parents find time to work hard and have fun? In our home it was work and pray. I rarely heard my parents laugh or saw them having fun. Fun was something we kids snuck in when our parents were not around. Now, I feel almost guilty cause we have so much fun—like I don't deserve it!"

"That's just the Catholic in you! Of course, you deserve fun! You have worked hard to get where you are, and that serious, hardworking nature of yours is not a bad thing. Hell, it is a good thing! I admire that about you. I think we just complement each other. You give me stability and purpose, and I give you fun. I see it like you were my missing piece to the puzzle, and I was yours."

Margaret looked at him in astonishment. He had a way of making everything so simple. But she knew he was absolutely right. She snuggled up to him and listened to his heartbeat, relishing in the light breeze coming through the window, gently caressing their bodies. A sense of peace engulfed her whole being.

Margaret loved Millarville and being part of a community. Her job as a teacher was much more rewarding than she even imagined. Her students loved how she mixed in art, and music, and poetry into every one of her subjects.

One evening during supper, Margaret told Rene about an idea she had for a science and social project.

"Rene, I'm thinking about starting an overnight camping trip program for the older kids at school. Some trips would be about nature. For example, we would take children on a hike and examine things like: identifying plants, rocks, bugs, animal tracks, and such, during the day. In the evening, we would teach them how to build a fire and how to cook their meals on the fire or in the ground with coals. Then before going to bed, we would teach them songs, and we would all sing by the campfire till bedtime."

"I love it, Margaret! But you're saying "we." Does that mean you want me to be part of it?"

"Yes, that is exactly what I mean. You have a lot more experience camping and all that. I think together we could make it really fun. And we would have parents volunteering to come along and help, too."

"Count me in. And I have another idea. What about learning about other cultures and ways of life around here, too, like taking a trip to the Big Buffalo Reserve and learning about their way of life? Or visiting a ranch? I don't know, but those are just a few ideas off the top of my head."

"I love it. I'm going to bring it up with the parents and the other teachers from Black Diamond and Turner Valley and see what they think. I'm sure if we put our brains together, we can come up with three or four trips a year."

The Millarville Market, which was started by the Millarville Race Club, had been operating since 1905, and was run by volunteers. Margaret and Rene had signed up to volunteer the first week they moved to Millarville. One morning after a beautiful summer's day at the market, Rene brought up the idea of getting an acreage.

"Wouldn't it be great to have our own little farm with chickens, a few cows, and a big vegetable garden? We could sell our produce here at the market. I miss the farm life, don't you?"

"Nope, I'm not interested."

"But, Margaret, please let's talk about it."

Anger rose in her chest. She was not going to get saddled down with a farm, and animals, and gardens and miss out on her dream. She had just started her singing and guitar lessons again, and she loved them. She spent hours thinking of how she could finally begin performing her songs in public.

"I knew this would happen!" she yelled.

"Whoa, what is this all about, Margaret. I have never seen you so angry. I don't like it at all."

"Don't like it? Well, too bloody bad! I thought you understood when you married me that once I had my teaching in place, I was going to start working on my music career. You knew that!"

"I'm not asking you to give up on your dream, just to postpone it for a bit. We can have it all, Margaret."

"You don't get it, do you. What a fool I have been."

A week went by, and Margaret did not talk to Rene the entire time. She could barely look at him. She slept in the living room on the couch and went over and over in her mind what a liar he was, and how he was just like all the other men, and once they got you, they changed.

Then on the seventh night, it hit her. She realized she wasn't mad at Rene; she was mad at herself for not being clear with him from the very beginning. She assumed he understood because he gave her a harmonica. It was her own fault for being so stupid as to believe it was a sign that he understood her. He didn't get her, nobody got her, ever, except maybe Aunt Bea. But it wasn't really fair to blame Rene.

It was five o'clock, and she was making supper. She heard a knock at the door and when she answered it, there was Rene wearing a red clown's nose. He was kneeling on one knee, holding a bouquet of hand-picked flowers in one hand, and a card in the other.

She couldn't help it; she had to smile. She opened the card. *I need you back, I can't live without you.* She looked at him and began to laugh.

"First of all, Rene, no cows. I milked enough growing up. But, yes, a garden would be great, and so would some laying hens."

"We could sell our veggies and eggs at the market; we could make our own goat-milk soap if we had goats," he said.

"I don't milk goats either!" she said with a smirk.

"I'll milk them, honey, I love milking goats."

"Okay, you can stand up now. "She grabbed him by the shirt, pulled him towards her, kissed him, and laughed.

The singing and guitar lessons she was taking would have to go on hold. She hated thinking about stopping them. They were expensive, but she was learning so much, and she was just starting to really discover what her voice was truly capable of. Her voice coach had told her it wasn't enough to have a love of music, it took work to train the voice.

At her second lesson he said, "Margaret, you have talent, there is no doubt about it. You have the love of music, too. And the songs you have written are good. But ideally, to get the whole package working, there are some things that we need to work on. First is your voice. We need to loosen it up, make it more flexible, build up your range, and bring more colour to your sound so you can bring in the emotions that you write about. To really succeed you have to get more power and control so when you sing your songs, people will have to stop and listen.

Secondly, I want you to really dig deep within yourself to write songs that come from your soul. Your songs are good, don't get me wrong, but every once in a while, I see glimpses of genius. It is that genius we want to nurture.

And lastly, if you're going to play guitar and harmonica, you need to find someone, other than me, to help you with your technique. You have the basics, but you need to excel. Does all this make sense?"

Margaret had found the advice so exciting and inspiring. She had been eager to finally be working on her lifelong goal. Now she cried on the phone when she told her coach that she had to quit her lessons. At least for a while.

She knew deep down that she didn't have the right to say no to the farm. Her life was great with Rene. They rarely fought; their sex life was fun; he showered her with compliments and gifts, and he was always kissing her and holding her hand. He was everything a woman would want in a husband, and their marriage was so much better than she could ever have imagined it could be. She thought about her mom and all the beatings she got, all the horrible names her father called her. She tried long and hard to recall if her father had said anything nice to her mother, or if she had ever seen them kiss or hug, and she couldn't think of one incident, not one.

Rene was the sweetest and most gentle man she had ever met, and she was luckier than most, she knew that for a fact. He found pleasure in the simplest things. Every meal she cooked him, he complimented her on it:

"Those are the best green peas I ever tasted, Margaret. You made that toast just right. Now what did you put on those pork chops? I don't think I ever tasted a pork chop that juicy."

He was not like her father or any other man or person she had ever met.

She applied at the local newspaper and got a part time job as a reporter and helped in the press room. She covered stories of events like the Strawberry Festival on the weekends. She also wrote the community column.

"Mr. and Mrs. Fournier had relatives visit them from Montmartre, Saskatchewan this weekend. Betty-Lou Stagg and her husband, Bob, celebrated the birth of their first child, Marion, born at Calgary General Hospital, July 2, 1942. Mrs. Bahr would like to invite everyone to a Come-And-Go Tea to celebrate her 75th birthday at the Legion Hall on Saturday. The 4-H Club is looking for volunteers for their fall fair event. Please call Sarah Boyce."

The job was interesting enough, and she enjoyed most of the work except when she had to cover music festivals. Interviewing musicians was hard. She was ashamed to admit it, but she was outright jealous of them.

Rene worked all the overtime he could get and was always being called to fix this or that for the neighbours. He was a handyman, and word got around quickly that he had a knack for fixing almost anything with a motor or anything electrical.

Their extra hard work paid off. Four years later, they got out of the car on a sunny spring morning, held hands, and smiled at one another as they walked towards their little farmhouse. Their little five-acre farm was just north of town off the same dirt road that Margaret had played her harmonica on years before. The house needed lots of repairs, but it had running water and an indoor toilet—no outhouse—a stipulation Margaret had made to Rene.

Rene had his list in his pocket and pulled it out.

"We will need to fix those front stairs right away and whitewash the exterior. You'll see what a fresh coat of paint will do. The barn we can leave for now till we get the goats."

"I love the red chicken coop, and oh, look, they left the hens. There must be ten of them!" Margaret said.

Inside the house, Margaret took a deep breath. Her heart felt so full. The kitchen was much bigger than she remembered when they had first looked at it. It was as clean as a whistle, and on top of the stove was a homemade apple pie that was still warm to the touch with a note.

Welcome to your new home. We hope you enjoy this house as much as we did. We planted the garden two weeks ago as a surprise, so enjoy! Call us if you have any questions, Mike and Susan.

Mike and Susan were in their eighties and were moving to a smaller home in town. They had their place up for sale for only a week when Rene found out about it from his boss, who was their son. They finally had enough money saved, and when he and Margaret looked at it, they knew instantly that it was meant to be. They paid cash.

Margaret walked to the garden and stared at the little seedlings that Mike and Susan had planted. They were popping out of the ground. Tears streamed down her face. Her mind drifted back to Nova Scotia. She saw herself working in the huge garden, enjoying the sun and the taste of the fresh carrots as she picked vegetables for hours. She felt the sun on her back and the faint smell of the salt air, and she could see the children playing Kick the Can by the barn and hear their laughter. She saw her sisters and herself in the summer kitchen, singing silly songs as they shelled and popped peas into their mouths as they worked. She saw her father give her a freshly butchered chicken, which she took into the house and cooked with the fresh tarragon she had picked in the garden, and then watched with delight as everyone ate, most of them asking for seconds. She saw her mother teaching her the secret that had been handed down from her own mother of how to make prickles crunchy, and how to make the perfect broth. She saw herself smile with pride when she put the last canned tomatoes on the shelf in the cellar. The beautiful memories played out before her eyes.

Without warning, grief overtook her. She doubled over onto the grass and began to sob uncontrollably. It was the first time she had allowed herself to feel the loss of her family. As she cried, she realized she had stuffed the beautiful memories of growing up on the farm deep inside and had only ever concentrated on the hurt and pain of her childhood. She realized then that Millarville, Rene, and their little acreage was home. Any regrets she had about working towards paying for their acreage disappeared completely in that moment.

As soon as they moved on to the farm, they invited their friends and neighbours over for a Friday Night Kitchen Party and the tradition began once again. When the weather was good, Ed and Lily, and Rene's brother Philip, came from Calgary.

Dear Auntie,

We are settling into the farmhouse so nicely! I wish you were here to see it. We have chickens, and in a month our goats are coming. Rene insists on making his own goat soap like his mother. Mike and Susan, who owned the place before us, planted the sweetest garden ever. It is as if they read my mind. I have all my favourite vegetables. The only thing I had to get were my herbs and garlic, which I'll plant in the fall. I can't tell you how nice it is to just putter in the garden and gather eggs. I realized as soon as we got here how much I missed living on a farm. Having your own produce and fresh eggs, there is nothing like it in the world. I love having my hands in the dirt and cooking with my home-grown ingredients! There is a sense of pride in it, I guess. I haven't given up entirely on my dream, but every penny we make is going towards the farm right now. There are so many renovations to do.

Everything I learned even in a short time with my singing coach has not gone to waste. I joined the community choir. Also, Rene and I started up kitchen parties at the farm. You wouldn't believe the response! We had ten people the first Friday, and the second Friday we had twenty! It is a good thing we have a big kitchen! There are several people from the Maritimes that have moved here to work in the oil fields and other people who just love to play music and dance. It is not a traditional kitchen party but a new invention. We teach each other folk songs from all over the world. There are lots of Europeans that have settled here so we have even learned folk songs in German and Ukrainian, and of course, lots of songs from Scotland and Ireland. We even have a Mr. and Mrs. Wong who own the Chinese restaurant who come. They said they can teach us some songs in Mandarin. They are so sweet, and the snacks they bring are delicious! So, I play my harmonica and guitar and sing every Friday night, and every Wednesday and Sunday, I sing in the community choir.

People always comment on my "beautiful" voice. It is nice to hear, but at the same time, when they say that, I feel an ache inside my chest. I'm not saying I'm not grateful for my life or that I'm not happy, cause I really, truly am. How can I not be? I have the best husband in the world, and a beautiful home, and I love teaching, and we have so many friends! But I feel in my heart that my dream is getting away from me and that makes me sad. But I try and not show it. I don't want to sound ungrateful for my life.

As expected, Rene's next request has been to start a family. I have to say, Auntie, I really hesitated because a child will really squash my dreams, but Rene kills me with his sweetness. I just can't seem to say no to him even if I try. I did tell him though that one was my limit, and I'll only agree if he promises not to pressure me for another one. He reluctantly agreed. So Auntie, we are actively trying. I guess if it happens it is meant to be.

I miss you terribly.

Love, Margaret

When Margaret finally agreed to start trying to get pregnant, Rene stepped up to the plate instantly.

"I'll cook dinner tonight just to show you that when you're busy with the baby, I'll do the cooking."

She raised her eyebrows and said, "Really?" Besides his Greek feasts that he made for special occasions; he had never cooked another meal.

He bought *The Ladies Auxiliary Cookbook* and followed it to the letter. If he didn't know how to do something, he would actually call on the cook who put the recipe in the book.

"Mrs. Nelson, Rene here, I'm making your apple pie recipe, and I don't understand what you mean by cutting the pastry. Can you explain it to me?"

The incident spread like wildfire as it does in a small town, and when it got to the community choir gang, they all laughed along with Margaret as she explained his reasoning for his new interest in cooking.

But she didn't tell them everything. Not about the candlelight suppers every weekend, or the record player he bought and their dancing to Bing Crosby and the Andrew Sisters in the living room late at night, or how their love making changed. Rene became much more serious and attentive to her wants instead of being his usual silly, fun self, making her laugh at all his goofy ideas of how or where they could have sex.

She loved the new Rene, but at the same time she missed him standing naked with a daisy in his mouth when she went to the barn, or his theatrical noises as she scratched his back as they made love, or his ridiculous made-up happy song after a particularly pleasant love making. She hoped some of that would make an appearance again occasionally.

1944-1945

It was November 22, 1944. Rene had stopped off at the post office in town on his way home for lunch. As he and Margaret were having their lunch, Rene opened the mail. His face turned ashen, and his eyes grew big.

"What? Oh my God, Margaret, I've been conscripted to go to war!"

"Conscripted? You mean you have to go?" Margaret asked in a panicked voice.

"Yes, even though I'm totally against the war, I have to go."

It was a shock. Up until then, Canada had not forced anyone to join the army. It was strictly voluntary, and Rene had no plan whatsoever to sign up. He was against conscription from the beginning, as were all his family back home.

Margaret stood on the train platform in Calgary watching her husband board the train in his uniform. She was trying to look composed and positive, but on the inside she was terrified. She had given up praying when she left the convent, but that day she was praying.

"Please God, bring him back safe, please, please."

In his first letter, he told her not to worry.

Once they realized I was a mechanic, I was deployed to France to work as a mechanic at the base camp. Margaret, I could not be in a safer place. It is hard work with not a day off and long hours, but they have good, hearty meals, and I'm so tired at the end of the day, I welcome my hard cot. I sleep well.

She felt better knowing he was in a safe place away from the fighting, but then in January he was sent home on sick leave. When Margaret saw him, she was shocked at how thin he was and how tired he looked. He had black circles under his eyes, and he winced in pain every move he made. He had been at the hospital in France with a bad case of shingles on the mid-section of his body, and his commander decided to send him home to rest for a month. She gently bathed him, and then put him to bed. He slept for two days without hardly moving. He was weak, exhausted, and in so much pain. It took a month to nurse him back to health and to where he looked like his old self. The day before he was to return to France, they made love for the first time since he had returned. It was gentle, quiet, and serious.

By September 5, 1945 he was home, and the war was over. On October sixth, baby Lena Bea, conceived on Rene's sick leave, was born at home in the farmhouse with a midwife from down the road. It was an easy birth, only four hours and "no tears or tears," the midwife told the family and friends that were waiting in the living room for Margaret's update. If it hadn't been for the cry of a baby, the guests would not have known Margaret had just given birth.

For a moment, as she lay with her beautiful daughter suckling at her breast, she wished her own mother was one of the guests in the living room along with Rene and his parents, his brother and her sister-in-law, and some friends. Looking into her daughter's eyes, she made a vow to her.

"Lena Bea, I love you more than I ever imagined I could love anyone. I promise to support and nurture your dreams and always be there for you."

IF I COULD LIVE AGAIN

Dear Auntie,

Rene and I had decided before the baby was born that if it were a girl, we would name her Lena Bea after Rene's mother, Madeline (who they call Lena), and you, dear Auntie. She is the most beautiful baby I have ever seen. She has flaming red hair just like you and me, but I don't think she has as many curls from what I can tell so far. Her beautiful curved-up mouth looks like she is always smiling (except when she is screaming, ha!), just like Rene's mouth. She was six pounds, five ounces She is so tiny! I forgot how tiny babies are, it has been so long since I have seen one. Please come and meet her! She is so precious.

I decided to take the whole year off from teaching to be a mom. I just can't imagine being away from her for a minute. But I have competition! Rene is over the moon in love with this child. I swear there isn't a man, woman, or child in all Millarville that does not know that he is the father to the most beautiful creature that ever lived. For a man who never smoked a day in his life, he has handed out more cigars than I can count. And, on top of that, he is a natural nurturer, which I always knew in my heart he would be. He jumps up to change her diaper. He rocks her to sleep as well as I do. And if he could figure a way to nurse her, he would! Dare I say, nothing like Father. I still remember one time when Ma and I and the rest of the girls went to town and left him at home with Hazel. She was only a few months old. When we came back, he was holding her at arms-length, and she had yellow poop running down her legs. He was so mad! He screamed at us for taking so long. He had no idea how to change a diaper, and he had ten children! Not only that, but here was a man who shoveled cow shit every day of his life, yet he was afraid of a little baby poop! I remember wanting to laugh at the absurdity, but of course I didn't dare.

I thought about coming to Nova Scotia when she gets around six months old. What do you think? I really want you to meet her and perhaps I can see some of my siblings again. Or maybe even Mother. Regardless, I'll send pictures as soon as we get them.

Love, Mommy Margaret

Dear Margaret,

Thank you so much for pictures of our precious little Lena Bea! She is beyond beautiful! I feel like I'm looking at you when you were a baby. She has your eyes and nose, but yes, I agree, her mouth does look like Rene's! I'm so happy for you. I'll come out one day, I'm not sure when. But now I have an extra incentive—my sweet Lena Bea!

I was surprised that you mentioned your mother. That is the first time. I guess having a child of your own changes one.

Something has happened that I feel I need to tell you about now that you mentioned your mother. I debated telling you but perhaps it is appropriate.

Last month, your mother called and asked if I could come out and give her a hand. She sounded terrible. Of course, I went out. She has rarely spoken to me since you left all those years ago, and so I thought it must be important.

Your father was in bed when I arrived, and your mother took me out to the barn to talk. She told me that the week before, your father had come after her with his fists in a rage for some ridiculous reason (her words). They had been rebuilding a wall in the barn, so there were two by four boards in the corner. She said something just came over her, and she just was not prepared to get another beating at her age for no good reason. She grabbed one of the two by four's and hit him square on the forehead. It just happened that there was a nail in the board, and it sliced his forehead good. She said there was blood everywhere! She got the bleeding stopped and put him to bed. She was shaking so bad when she told me, Margaret. I really felt for her. It was the first time she ever stood up to him she told me, but she said she just couldn't take another beating.

I told her she did the right thing and that she should have done it long ago.

I went with her to the bedroom and saw your father, his head all bandaged up. He woke up when we walked in, and when he saw me, he began to cry. Can you believe it? I wouldn't if I hadn't seen it with my own eyes. He told me he was sorry about the way he had treated you and the rest of the kids, and his wife, and me, and he promised never to hurt anyone again.

Back in the kitchen, I told your mother that it sounded like she had finally knocked some sense into him and that made us both laugh a little at the irony.

Now, whether he keeps his promise, we shall have to wait and see. I know it is a pattern with him. He apologizes to your mother after the beatings, and then she forgives him and they're all fine and dandy again till the next one. But I don't have to tell you that. I guess the difference is that she fought back this time. Will it make a difference? I guess only time will tell.

I helped your mom with the cows, as the only children left at home now are the twin boys, and to be honest, they seem as useful as tits on a boar. Your mother had to yell at them constantly as they were always running off chasing each other and fooling around. They never lifted a hand to help with supper, and they had to be told, I swear, a hundred times, to milk the cows before they finally listened. Your ma and I were working like dogs. Hard to believe they are related to you! I have gone out every chance I get to give her a hand these last two weeks. Sadly, from what I gathered; it seems most of your siblings don't come home to visit once they have left home. Louise is the only one that I know of who comes by on a regular basis. She lives down the road. She married a McKinnon boy—nice man from what I hear—quiet like Louise apparently. Your mother told me she hasn't been able to come to help her, as she just had a set of twins. Two little identical girls that look exactly like their papa. No red hair! Lucy and Maggie were born one month ago, so her hands are full. I haven't met them yet, but your mother says they are good little babies. We are planning to go together to visit them next week. Maybe this is old news, as I know Louise and you do correspond back and forth. She is such a nice person. A gentle soul really.

Your father can work now, so I haven't gone out since yesterday. I'll keep you up to date, but only if you wish. Maybe a trip home might do some good. Perhaps mend some broken hearts, yours and your mother's, anyway. The jury is still out on your father!

Kiss that sweet baby from me.

Love, Great Auntie Bea

As Margaret read her aunt's letter, she felt her chest tighten. Could it be that her father changed and that her mother finally stood up for herself? She never thought she'd see the day. She looked down at her nursing daughter and felt her body relax instantly. She smiled at how she kept falling asleep and stopped sucking only to start up again and again. It was so cute. She could watch her little face all day. Margaret loved nursing. She loved the way that

Lena Bea would look right into her eyes and hold her finger as she suckled. She rocked her to sleep singing to her till her sweet little eyes would close. She wondered if her mother felt like that with her when she was an infant? Did she love me as much as I love Lena Bea? If so, why did she not show it? If she even felt a quarter of the love she felt for Lena Bea, it would have been enough. But as she sat and thought back over her childhood, she just did not recall any evidence of real love. The closest was when she gave her her father's harmonica. If she ever did see her mother again, she had so many questions that she would like to ask her. Like why she didn't love her, or if she did, why she didn't show it? She realized as she sat there that she never really wondered if her father ever loved her. She was dead sure that he was incapable of feeling love for anyone.

It hit her like a ton of bricks that she would never know the reasons why her parents were the way they were. Two people with twelve children and incapable of demonstrating love. It was pathetic. One thing she did know was that she was not ready to forgive her parents. Not yet anyway. Perhaps later. Perhaps never. Right now, in the moment, she was loving her life with Rene and their baby. It was all she needed. As wise Auntie Beatrice told her years before: we only have the moment, and her moment was awesome. Reliving the story of her past did nothing but bring up pain. She was not going back to Nova Scotia.

1953

Margaret and Lena Bea stood on the train station platform in Calgary eagerly waiting for the train to arrive. Lena Bea was doing cartwheels on the platform. Her little pink dress was already full of dirt and grime, and she had only been in it for two hours. Margaret wondered how in God's green earth she could get so dirty. The child could not sit still if she tried. She was determined for Lena Bea to look her best for Aunt Beatrice, but somehow, she managed to look like the last rose of summer.

"Lena Bea! Come here. Quit jumping around for one minute!"

Margaret put a little spit on her finger and tried to rub the dirt off Lena Bea's face. She straightened out the bow on her dress, and then sighed. It was impossible. She was so tired of scolding her. She blamed Rene for the child's wild behaviour. He let her get away with everything and anything, while she was always the bad parent who did the disciplining.

"Is Aunt Beatrice old like with grey hair and stuff?

"No, Lena Bea, I'm sure she has some grey hair, but she is only sixty-four years old.

"That sounds old to me. How come I'm named after her? Do you think she likes making cookies? I thought maybe we could make cookies. Or maybe she can play catch with me?"

"Lena Bea, you ask a lot of questions. Why not just try and slow down a bit and quit hopping around like a jack rabbit? Oh, look, the train is coming…"

Margaret watched as Aunt Beatrice gingerly stepped down while holding onto the railing. She had on a green-and-white floral dress and lugged a huge leather bag that looked to be half her size. She looked so tiny and Lena Bea was right, she did indeed have a bit of grey hair around her temples, but the rest of her hair was coiled into a braided bun and was still bright red. It had been thirteen years since the wedding; that was when Margaret had last seen her, and though she looked older, what Margaret found really shocking was that she also looked far rounder and shorter than she remembered.

"Auntie!!!" she yelled as she walked quickly with her arms outstretched. "You're finally here! You look magnificent!"

She closed her eyes as she hugged her aunt, taking in her comforting, earthy smell.

"Oh, it is so good to see you!"

"And I'm so happy to finally be here!"

When she opened her eyes, she saw a woman in a red checkered dress. The woman looked like her mother.

"Ma?"

Standing sheepishly behind Aunt Beatrice was her mother, looking strangely quite stylish.

"Ma? Is that you?"

Her aunt stepped aside, and Mary stepped towards her daughter, took her hands in hers, and looked into her eyes and said, "Hello, Margaret, I hope you don't mind the surprise. Beatrice talked me into coming."

Eight-year-old Lena Bea, who had been standing behind her mother, grabbed Mary's dress and tugged on it.

"Hi, are you my grandma?"

"Yes, I am sweetheart. That is if you're the famous Lena Bea I have been hearing all about."

"Yes, I'm Lena Bea Gallant of Millarville, Alberta."

She then turned to Beatrice. "Are you Great Auntie Beatrice?" she asked.

"Yes, I am, sweetie. Nice to finally meet you in person!"

"You two kind of look alike. And you have the same hair as me and mom. Grandma, are you moving here, too?"

"No, I'm not, I just came for a visit and to finally meet you."

Lena Bea grabbed her great aunt's hand and her grandmother's hand and said, "Okay, let's go, I want to show you my room, and you know we have goats and chickens, right? Well, it is your lucky day because Papa is making soap today, so you can help me and my best friend Jim, he lives next door, don't worry you'll meet him, and he's really nice. Well, Jim and I, we stack the soap up and get them ready to sell at the market on Saturday. What is your favourite smell? I love lavender, do you?"

Margaret grabbed their bags, then walked up to the station porter and asked him to help with getting the rest of the luggage. She walked quickly to catch up with the three of them. Lena Bea was chatting with her grandmother and great aunt, rarely waiting for them to answer the million questions she asked them. Margaret followed them in silence to the car. Her mother looked back at her and winked, then mouthed "so sweet" as she glanced down at Lena Bea.

Margaret felt her heart pounding. She didn't know what she was feeling, happiness or fear? She wasn't quite sure. But there right in front of her was her Ma, who she hadn't seen since the day she left for the convent on her sixteenth birthday. The day her mother gave her the harmonica. That was twenty years ago. How did Aunt Beatrice pull this off? How had her father ever let her go? Perhaps he had changed. Or was it that her mother had changed? She did look different. Older, yes, but there was something else. The fear embedded in the lines of her mouth and her forehead was gone. Yes, perhaps that was it. In fact, her face looked pleasant, almost peaceful, and the permanent frown Margaret remembered seemed to have disappeared, and in its place was a slight grin. Even her eyes seemed to twinkle. She was actually beautiful, Margaret decided. It was funny but her Ma and Aunt Bea looked much more alike now than she ever remembered. The only difference Margaret really noticed as she walked behind them was that Aunt Bea was plump and waddled as she walked, whereas her mother was slim, strong, and muscular, and walked with a purpose.

As they sat down for supper, Beatrice laughed as she told them why she had decided to move to Millarville.

"Well, if you're going to name your child after me, then I thought to myself, I guess I'd better get to know her. I know I'm a little late, but better late than never. The retirement thing is not for me. Sitting around playing cards and freezing your arse off all winter long and shoveling snow and the like, just wasn't doing much for me. Six months of retirement nearly made me crazy. So here I am. I always said I would come! Now, I don't expect to move in with you, as I have my quirks from living alone all these years, but I do expect to spend a lot of time with Lena Bea."

Lena Bea smiled as she shoveled potatoes into her mouth.

Margaret looked over at her, "Lena Bea, honey, slow down and chew your food, it is not a race."

"But Jim and I wanna take Grandma and Auntie to see the chickens. They haven't seen them yet."

"There is plenty of time, don't worry."

"Tell me about this old folk's home you wrote me about," interrupted Beatrice.

"It's not an old folks' home. It is called the Foothills Senior Village, and it is just down from Main Street. I checked them out and the apartments are tiny but gorgeous. There is a common area where you can play cards, and they have dances and entertainment and pot-luck suppers. It is such a great idea. And I know you will miss gardening, but our little acreage is yours. You can plant anything you want. It could use more flowers."

"Thanks, sweetie, the senior's place sounds perfect. As for flowers, I hate to say it, but yes, you need a little more colour in your yard. I'll get right on that while there is still some time. Next year we will have this place looking like it should be in a magazine," she said as she clapped her hands to her thighs.

Margaret felt a little strange talking to Aunt Bea with her mother right there.

It was so obvious to anyone who might be watching that Margaret and her aunt were very close. They knew each other's darkest secrets; they knew about each other's hopes and dreams; they had a history, whereas she had very little history with her own mother. There was not the bond with her mother that Margaret and her aunt shared. And no matter how hard Margaret tried to include her mother in conversations, it was difficult. But Margaret watched her mother, and she didn't look distressed. She seemed genuinely happy to listen and laugh along with everyone.

That evening when everyone was in bed, Margaret sat in the living room in her rocking chair, looking out the window at the night sky. It was a habit she had when she couldn't sleep—to look at the stars and the moon and to listen to the crickets and frogs.

"Margaret?"

It was her mother's voice. She turned to see her standing there in a floral housecoat and the moccasins Margaret had bought for Aunt Bea because she knew she would not like the wooden floors in the farmhouse.

"Ma, trouble sleeping? Can I get you a chamomile tea with honey?"

"That would be lovely. The time change is not easy, and all the excitement makes it hard to calm my mind."

"I'm sure it is difficult to shut off all the thoughts that must be running around in your head. I'm having the same problem—minus the time change," she said as she placed the tea pot on the table with two teacups.

"Mother, I just want to say how happy I am to have you here. It was a real shock to see you. I wondered if I would ever see you again," Margaret said, hoping she could hold back the tears.

"I know, I was worried, too, but Beatrice, who has been a godsend to me in more ways than one, assured me it would all work out, and she was right. I have changed, Margaret. It took a long time to stand up to your father and when I finally did, I was so mad at myself for not doing it earlier. I mean I could have killed him. I was so mad and fed up, but thankfully he didn't die. But it did smarten him up. He is a changed man, Margaret, and he said he wanted me to tell you that he was so sorry for the way he treated you growing up."

"I have to be honest I find it hard to believe he has changed. He was a monster. But I guess I have to take your word for it." She paused for a second before she continued. "Can I ask you a personal question?"

"Yes, anything."

"What did you ever see in him?"

"Margaret, I know it is hard to believe, but he was charming at first. He told me stories about his awful childhood with his stepdad beating him all the time and locking him the cellar for days. I felt sorry for him, and I thought that he just needed to be loved and he would be the opposite of his stepfather. So silly, I know. I see it now. He was so kind and loving and a real romantic while we were dating. But once we got married, it was like a light switch turned on, and he began to show his mean streak. When I was pregnant with you, I thought I would lose you because I got such a lickin' when I was seven months pregnant that I ended up in hospital. My parents wanted to take me home. But he came to the hospital and was so remorseful and he promised never to do that again. I believed him. But as you know, it just got worse as the years went on. And you, Margaret, got the worst out of all the children. The twin boys at the end, I don't think they ever got a lickin' at all. He was so hard on you. He was so determined to have a boy first off and when you came along, he was mad at the world. And then all he ever got were girls until the last twins. I don't want to make excuses for him, Margaret. That is the last thing I would ever do. But I was too weak from my own beatings, and busy raising all you kids, and being pregnant so much, and working on the farm that I just... I guess I gave up trying to defend you. It is no excuse. I'm so very sorry for all you went through."

"Thanks for saying that. It is okay, Ma. I've learned that my past made me a strong person and more determined to be the opposite of Father, and yes, even you, to be honest. Aunt Bea was really the one to help me see that in a strange way, my childhood made me into a capable woman."

Mary gently put her hand on top of Margaret's. "You certainly have turned into a wonderful, strong woman, and you have a beautiful family. Rene seems like such a sweet and gentle man. And your little whirlwind, Lena Bea, is a very special little girl. She reminds me of you. She has the same determination as you had when you were her age. I'm so happy for you, Margaret. I truly am," Mary said as she looked into Margaret's eyes.

"Thanks, Ma," she said as she poured another cup of tea into their cups. "Now let's change the subject. Tell me all about my siblings. They are all so bad at writing letters. I only hear from some of them when someone dies or has a baby."

"Well, let's see…"

They sat together at the kitchen table, sipping tea and chatting into the wee hours of the morning. If someone were to eavesdrop, they would have noticed that Margaret and her mother had the same laugh, and they would have heard them crying when they were talking about the death of two of her sisters: sweet little Annie to scarlet fever at the age of twelve, and Helen, who was killed in a bomb attack overseas in the medical facility where she was nursing men coming from the front lines.

Beatrice woke up and came into the kitchen. She saw Rene standing at the counter, gazing at the wall.

"Good morning, Rene." He didn't answer. She walked up to him and put her hand on his shoulder.

"Good morning, Rene," she said again, looking at his eyes to try and see what he was staring at. As far as she could tell, it was the tile on the wall. She patted his shoulder again.

"Are you all right, sweetie?"

He finally looked over at her.

"Good morning, Beatrice. How was your sleep?"

"Very good, thank you. Slept like a log."

Margaret walked into the kitchen and went over to her aunt and gave her a kiss on the cheek.

"You're up. I hope Ma and I didn't keep you awake, we talked for a long-time last night."

"I did hear you off and on, but I was so tired I would just fall back asleep again. I'm so happy you two got to chat alone."

Margaret sat down with a cup of coffee across from her aunt.

"I can't believe I am sitting having coffee with you! It is like a dream come true," she said, looking into her aunt's smiling eyes.

Rene walked over to Margaret and kissed her on top of her head and said "I gotta go to work, you gals have a wonderful day."

"Bye, honey."

Beatrice poured herself another coffee and sat down at the table.

"I was a little nervous about the surprise visit, Margaret, but deep down I knew how important it was to heal old wounds ever since I visited George in Toronto. It's funny how life is. I was reading Ralph Waldo Emerson a week before I left, and I came across a passage that said, 'You cannot do a kindness too soon, for you never know how soon it will be too late.' It was that quote that made me reach for the phone and call Mary and insist she come along. It was like the universe was sending me a message. Your mother said yes without missing a beat."

"Well, you were right as usual. I'm so happy she is here. I feel like a weight I have carried around most of my life has somehow been lifted off my shoulders. I don't know how else to describe it. I feel light. Like I'm floating on a cloud."

That afternoon, they drove to town. When they got out of the car, without a thought, they all held hands—Lena Bea in between her grandmother and great aunt, and Margaret on the end, holding her mother's hand. They walked down Main Street in Millarville grinning from ear to ear, greeting folks and introducing Beatrice and Grandma Mary to their friends and people in town. It was a sight to see. Three generations with the same flaming red hair, Margaret at six foot one, Beatrice and Mary at five foot two, and little Lena Bea, half the size of her great aunt and grandmother. There was not a town folk who didn't take a second look at the four of them as they sauntered down the streets of the little town, shopping for groceries and bedding plants.

Later that day, Rene walked into the kitchen. Mary and Margaret were chopping vegetables and laughing and singing. Lena Bea and Beatrice were at the kitchen table, wearing the matching aprons Rene had bought for them. Flour flew in the air as they sprinkled the table, laughing and smiling.

"What are you two doing?" Rene asked Beatrice and Lena Bea.

"We're making apple strudel, Papa. Look, we're going to stretch the flour across the whole entire table! Ma got the recipe and instructions from Mrs. Schmidt. I wanted to have it for dessert because Mrs. Schmidt always gives it to me when we visit, and it is sooo good, Papa."

"Well, it looks like you will be able to feed the whole town!" Rene said with a laugh.

"She is amazing," Mary whispered to Beatrice as they sat in the centre table of the Irish pub in Calgary, listening to Margaret singing and playing her guitar and harmonica to the crowd.

Near the end of her last set many of the patrons were clearly drunk, and Margaret heard men making crude comments about her, as usual.

"Hey, Red, come home with me and sing me to sleep."

"Wrap those braids around me, and give me a kiss, Red."

Margaret had been performing at the pub for two years on Thursday nights, and it was the part she hated the most. This time though, instead of feeling anger, she felt a wave of embarrassment.

"I should have warned Ma and Auntie that this is the usual response from the audience as the men get drunker and drunker," she thought.

As she was packing up her gear, her Ma and Aunt came up to the stage.

"Margaret, that was so wonderful. I just never imagined how good you were. I am so proud," her mom said, with Beatrice nodding as she talked.

"Yes, it was incredible. I loved it!"

"Thanks. But I really want to apologize for not warning you about the drunks. I am so embarrassed that you had to witness that." Her face was straining to smile.

"Is it always like that?" asked Beatrice

"I'm afraid so. Sometimes a lot worse. I've decided that after tonight I am done. I have put up with it for too long, and having you both here and listening to that was a wake-up call."

"But what will you do? You can't stop performing. You are too good," said her mother.

"Don't worry, I won't stop. I can do other types of gigs. I can perform in places where people actually listen to my songs and aren't just there to get drunk. Come on, let's go home."

She called her agent the next day and told him to only book her soft seaters like concert halls and festivals from now on. He wasn't impressed. He told her she was a hard sell. She told him either find her some decent gigs or he was fired. And she hung up on him.

As they sat on the bench at the train station, Margaret noticed Lena Bea reaching for her grandmother's hand. With a weak, sad smile, Mary gently stroked Lena Bea's hand and kissed it gently. It was bittersweet. She couldn't remember if her mother had ever rubbed or kissed her hand like that. At the same time, it was so wonderful to see how Lena Bea had stolen her mother's heart over the last few weeks. Margaret finally broke the silence.

"Well, gals, it was quite the three weeks, wasn't it? We got Aunt Beatrice moved into her little senior's apartment, and dare I say, it was so much fun decorating it. And all the shopping and cooking meals together, wasn't that just the best? Ma, what was your favourite thing we did?"

Mary looked at Margaret, and her eyes were teary. "Too many, too many, just too many wonderful times," she said, her voice quivering.

"I know, sister, we have had some of the best times I think I have ever had. But I must say, dancing the jig with you at the kitchen party was a real hoot. Don't think I'll get that image out of head anytime soon!"

They all began to laugh.

Margaret flashed back to the kitchen party. She remembered the feeling that came over her as she watched her mother that night. It was like watching a different person. She was funny and engaging with everyone, and she was laughing and singing, and yes, when she and Aunt Beatrice performed a jig duet for the group that they used to perform as children, they had the crowd laughing, and clapping, and hooting, and howling. She had never seen her mother or aunt dance a jig and had no idea that they even could.

The train arrived at seven a.m. sharp and when it was time to hug her mother, she embraced her until she could feel her begin to soften and recip- rocate. It was the hug that Margaret had longed for her whole life. When Margaret finally let go, her mother stood on her tiptoes and pulled her daughter towards her and kissed her on her forehead. Margaret began to cry, and as the conductor shouted: "All aboard!" her cries turned into sobs.

Lena Bea grabbed Margaret's hand and looked up at her. 'Don't worry, Ma, we'll see her again."

But Margaret had a feeling deep down that that was the last time she would ever see her mother. Rene, Margaret, Lena Bea, and Aunt Beatrice waved till the train turned the corner and was out of sight. As they drove back to Millarville no one spoke. The only sound was Margaret whimpering in the back seat.

Aunt Bea opened the door to her little apartment.

"Come in, I was just sitting down to have my tea. I didn't know you were coming over today."

"I just dropped Lena Bea off at baseball practice, so I thought I would swing by and see how you were making out," said Margaret.

"It's Thursday, don't you have to go play your gig in Calgary soon?"

"I quit."

"You said you were going to quit, but I wasn't sure you would right away."

"Yup. I am done with that place. The pub has been a good gig in a lot of ways. It has been a great place to play my new songs and play alone in front of an audience. But I have a problem with all the drunks and the crude comments. You heard them the night you came. And that was mild. I have had some scary moments. I have never told anyone this, not even Rene, but I have even punched out a man who was trying to grab me as I walked to my car after a show. I mean, I really lost it and punched him out! He was bleeding in a heap on the road. I have never hit anyone in my life. I was so ashamed that I completely lost it like that. I went way too far, but the rage overtook me. It was like I was not in my body. It reminded me of Father when he lost it on us. I remember his anger turned on like a switch that could not be turned off till he was done. That is how I felt. I'm so ashamed. I just can't believe I did that. I could have killed him."

"Oh, Margaret, I'm so sorry that you went through that. Everyone, and I mean every single human being on this earth, has a shadow side. It is that hidden aspect of yourself that holds your pain and your fears. It can be confusing. Given certain circumstances, like being attacked like you were, you act from your shadow side. In a way it is instinctual, "fight or be killed." It is important to recognize that."

"You mean it was okay what I did? Cause it didn't feel good."

"You defended yourself. Did you go too far? That is the part that you need to explore some more. Given your upbringing, I would guess there is a great deal of anger hidden deep inside you. You can't ignore that. But for now, all you can do is learn from it, and maybe next time if it ever happens again, you may still defend yourself but perhaps not go too far. I don't know."

"You always have a way of seeing things that I never would have even imagined. How do you know all this stuff?"

"I taught school to teenagers for the last thirty-seven years—and I'm old. Old people know stuff. Ha!"

"You know I have been hanging onto that shame for a year. One conversation with you and I already feel like the that shame has been lifted. Gosh, it is good to have you here in person!"

"Well, it is great to be here." Aunt Beatrice said as she poured more tea into their cups. "Now tell me, sweetie, what is your new plan of action?"

"I have been trying to really work on my contacts so I can get some soft seater gigs, and I've submitted tons of applications for festivals for this coming summer."

"What is a soft-seater gig?"

"It is like a concert hall or festival where people come to hear you perform, a place where people are not talking and half listening or drinking themselves silly."

"A new word for me. I like the sound of that."

"Jack, my promotor, is not the greatest, though. I think I have to let him go. It took a long time to find someone who would even consider promoting me, though. I was turned down by so many of them because I'm a woman, and I play guitar, and harmonica, and write my own songs, and, if you can believe it, because I'm tall! I mean I have heard every excuse in the world."

"I always knew it would be hard for you, Margaret, but I never imagined it would be that hard."

"I know, it's crazy. Consequently, I do a lot of my own leg work."

"Well, good for you."

"Yeah, I actually have a meeting next week in Calgary with Dixie Bill. Have you heard him on the radio, Dixie Bill and the Range Riders?

"Yes, I think I have. You told me about them a while ago."

"Well, when I heard they were coming to Calgary, I called up the radio station and got them to give me Bill's phone number. When I called Bill, I told him I was an undiscovered singer-songwriter looking to make it in the music industry and that I wanted to learn the ropes. Bill was so kind and said he would love to meet me. So, I'm going. I haven't told Rene yet, though. I don't know how he will react. He has been acting so strange lately. I honestly don't know what's wrong with him. So to be honest, I've put off telling him."

"Sweetie, that is great news! I'm here to look after Lena Bea, so take your time. I'm so excited for you!" Aunt Beatrice said as she raised her tea cup and clinked Margaret's.

"Thanks. I'm excited. The hard part is deciding which songs to perform for him. I have enough songs written to fill a drawer."

"Well, I really liked that one about lovin' your smiling face. It is so catchy even the drunks were singing along at the pub! Ha!"

"Oh, yes, "Your Smiling Face" that would be a great one. I wrote it about Rene, you know."

"I guessed as much. And speaking of Rene. I don't mean to be nosy, but I, too, have noticed some odd behaviour and have been meaning to ask you if he is all right? He seems different to me, for lack of a better word, a little lost perhaps?"

"Yeah, I know, I have been kind of ignoring it, I'm afraid, as I have been so busy with Lena Bea and her crazy schedule and my obsession with my music career. But yes, I agree, he hasn't been himself though he hasn't mentioned anything to me about feeling different. Maybe I should make an appointment with Dr. Ingles for him. I feel so selfish now that you mentioned it."

"Oh, sweetie! You're not selfish just preoccupied. You have a lot on your plate. I'm sure Rene will be okay. I'm here to help with Lena Bea, so no worries there. I just can't get enough of that busy little girl. She just does not stop, does she?"

"She is a handful. She is into so many sports, and a year and half ago she started fiddle lessons thanks to her Uncle Philip, who has been encouraging her since she was six to play the with him. Just what we needed, more activities! I just don't know how to keep up with her busy schedule. And she is so stubborn, and driven, and talented! If she wasn't so good at everything she does, I would get her to cut out some activities, but she really is a good athlete. I have been told by her coaches that she is Olympic material—can you believe it? I don't know how they can tell that an eight-year-old is

Olympic material. And while she can't sing worth a damn, she sure can play that fiddle. Well, you heard her. She is a natural! Even Philip, who has been playing all his life, said she surpassed him in a year of lessons. Her new thing this week is that she wants to learn more about jazz—can you believe it?

"Jazz and the Olympics!" her aunt laughed and slapped her leg. "She is something special that girl. You and Rene have done a wonderful job."

"Well, I don't know about me doing such a great job. Rene is the one who should get most of the credit. He has spent so much time with her, playing sports, driving her here and there, talking to her coaches, and playing basketball and baseball with her all the time. He is so great with her, and with kids in general. As I'm sure you've noticed, Jim, the boy next door, almost lives here. He is such a sweet boy. Rene adores him. He is like the son he never had."

"I noticed that. Such a nice young boy, so polite, too."

"His dad lost both his legs in the war and also suffers badly with depression. His mom is really nice, but she has to work so hard to keep a roof over their heads and to try to care for her husband. I feel so bad for her."

"Poor woman. I can't imagine."

"I sometimes feel guilty for wanting so much more in my life when I see someone like her. She has so many obstacles she has to deal with daily that any dreams she may have had in her life have surely been squashed," Margaret said.

"You can't think that way, Margaret. We are all on our own journey. You have a gift to give the world. The world needs music. It is such an important part of the fabric of our society, and as Plato once said, 'Music gives a soul to the universe, wings to the mind, flight to the imagination and life to everything.' One of my favourite quotes!"

"Oh, Auntie, when I saw you step down from the train, I just knew that the universe was shining down on me again! I have missed our long talks—and your quotes!" Margaret laughed.

"I'm here for you and our little whirlwind Lena Bea, and for Rene, too. You just see what this meeting brings with Dixie Bill, and what Dr. Ingles has to say about Rene, and we will deal with one day at a time. I'm not going anywhere."

The day before she was to leave for Calgary to meet Dixie Bill, Rene asked her if she had noticed the "button people" in the living room.

"The button people?"

"Ya, in the living room; the mama is on the couch, the papa is in the armchair, and the two children are on the floor playing."

"Rene, what are you talking about? Are you joking?"

"You don't see them?" he asked with a serious face and a look in his eyes that Margaret did not recognize. Rene went on to describe the button people. They had buttons for eyes and noses but no mouths. They had straw for feet and hands. They were dressed in black, and they did not talk.

"I know it sounds strange, Margaret, but… are you sure you don't see them?"

"Yes, I'm sure I don't see them, but that doesn't mean they are not real," she said cautiously.

He was starting to get agitated, and the look in his eyes scared her. Then, like a switch turned off in his brain, he stared at the wall and looked a million miles away.

Margaret called their doctor.

"He has been acting so strange lately, and now these "button people" hallucinations. I guess I was so preoccupied with my own plans, my mother's visit, my aunt moving here, and Lena Bea that I didn't want to admit that something was going on with him. I'm so ashamed. I also noticed that he is getting clumsy, and he has never been clumsy. It's like his hands and feet are not working. He drops things, trips when he walks, and he is not sleeping well at all. God, now that I say it out loud it sounds serious. Doc, I'm so worried."

"Can you bring him in tomorrow, Margaret? We need to check this out right away, it doesn't sound like Rene at all," Dr. Ingles said.

Dr. Ingles had been friends with Rene for six years. They curled together, and they often won every bonspiel they played in.

Margaret cancelled her meeting in Calgary with Dixie Bill, and she took Rene to the doctor instead.

Two months later, after Rene saw three specialists, Dr. Ingles called them into his office.

"Margaret and Rene, I'm afraid I have bad news. After all the tests and consultations, we are positive it is Lewy Body Dementia. It is, I'm sorry to say, a fatal type of dementia where visual hallucinations, delusions, memory deterioration, and movement worsen until finally death occurs," he explained.

"Oh, my God," Margaret said quietly.

She knew it wasn't going to be good news, but the diagnosis was much worse than anything she had imagined.

"It is a rare type of dementia that was discovered in 1912, and so it has been known about for a long time. It is a blend of Parkinson's and dementia characterized by visual hallucinations. I'm familiar with it, fortunately. I say fortunately because being that it is quite rare, the chances of diagnosing it so quickly are unheard of. When I had my practice in Calgary, I had another patient with it, and it took over two years to properly diagnosis him. There were many incorrect diagnoses first: Parkinson's Disease, prostate cancer, and even schizophrenia. It was a nightmare going to different specialists, and the opioid medication that we tried only made everything worse and seemed to create more stress. So, in one way, we are very lucky to not have to go through all that. The specialists have confirmed my suspicions."

"How long do I have?" Rene asked in a flat voice.

"Three to five years. We just don't know for sure."

"But he's only thirty-seven, how can he have dementia? I thought that was for old people?" Margaret asked, shocked.

"There are many types of dementia; it is a large category, and to be truthful, we don't know the cause of most of them, but Lewy Body Dementia we do know often shows up in younger people. I'm so very sorry."

They left the doctor's office holding hands. Rene was shaking like a leaf from head to toe. Tears streamed down Margaret's face as she drove them home.

"There are no pills, and no cure," the doctor's words kept repeating over and over in Margaret's head.

"So, am I just supposed to watch him deteriorate before my eyes? There has to be something I can do!" she thought.

That evening, as Margaret sat at her kitchen table opening the mail that had been piling up over the last two weeks, she eyed an envelope that came from the Calgary Kiwanis Music Festival.

"Probably another rejection letter," she thought.

"Dear Margaret Gallant,

It is with great pleasure that you have been accepted to play at the Calgary Kiwanis Music Festival 1953, in the category of "Stars of Tomorrow" on stage three. Your set is twenty-five minutes. Here is what you will need. . . Please confirm."

Her hands trembled. She folded her arms on the table, dropped her head down, and began to sob.

"After all these years, I finally get my big break. Finally! But how the bloody hell can I accept with all that we're going through?"

She raised her head, wiped the tears from her eyes with the sleeve of her housecoat, then slapped her cheeks. "Snap out of it."

She took a sip of her crab apple wine and re-read the letter one more time before tossing it into the garbage can.

The "button people" stayed with Rene, but he didn't seem scared of them. He explained to Margaret that they mostly just sat there on the couch in the living room or followed him around. Margaret noticed that he seemed to get used to them. One day as they were walking in town doing errands, she asked him if they had disappeared because he hadn't mentioned them in a few days.

In a flat voice he said, "No, they are over by the picnic bench now."

The other symptoms started to take their toll and he had to quit work. He became clumsier, and more forgetful, and he had trouble sleeping. His gait became worse, and he seemed more confused as the months went by. Then a year later, he began to wander away.

"Where are you going, honey?" Margaret asked as she watched Rene get up off the couch and grab his jacket, putting it over his pajamas. It was nine o'clock in the evening, and she had just finished giving him a bath. He had seemed pretty good. As she washed his back, she began to sing "La Bastringue," the first Acadian song he ever taught her, and by the second verse he was singing along, not missing a beat or confusing the verses. It was a sweet moment, hearing him sing again.

"I'm going to work now."

Margaret didn't like to tell him he was wrong, as that seemed to upset him these days. So she said the first thing that came into her mind.

"Oh, honey, I'm sorry, I forgot to tell you, they closed the garage today, as Derrick had to go to a doctor's appointment in Calgary. Why not just enjoy the day off? Come sit beside me here," she said as she padded the seat beside her on the couch.

It worked. She was learning. She sighed with relief as he came over, still in his jacket, and sat next to her, without saying a word, and stared at the wall.

The saddest day came six months later. "Who's that?" he asked as Lena Bea sat down at the table for breakfast. The look on Lena Bea's face was horrific. She turned all red, and her mouth dropped, and she looked at her mother for a cue, not knowing what to say.

Margaret closed her eyes briefly, and then took a deep breath and said "That is your daughter, Lena Bea."

"Oh! Well, I'll be, I have a daughter now?"

Lena Bea got up from the table and went to her bedroom. Margaret could hear her muffled cries. She went to her room, sat down next to her on the bed, and put her arm around her.

"Honey, I'm so sorry."

"I can't believe he doesn't know me, Mom! I just don't understand how this can be happening! It's like he is disappearing before our eyes! Where is he going, Mom?"

"I don't know where he is going. I don't understand it either. I wish I knew. Today it is you, tomorrow it may be me he forgets. I only know it is going to get a whole lot worse, and there is nothing we can really do about it except love him and help him as best as we can as he deteriorates."

"I want my papa back!" she sobbed

"I know, honey, I know," she said as she rubbed her back. "You know, wise Aunt Bea once told me: when things are bad, the best thing to do is just breathe. Just sit there and watch your breath go in and out. She taught me that we can't change anyone else or situations sometimes, we can only change ourselves and how we react and respond to them. She said, 'Margaret, when you're in a really bad situation, always remember that there is only one thing in life that you really have to do, and that is breathe.'"

Lena Bea took long, deep breaths. Her sobbing started to slow down.

"That a girl."

She took Lena Bea's face into her hands. "Honey, I never told you much about my childhood, but my father beat me a lot, and sometimes so bad that he broke my ribs, and twice he dislocated my shoulder. I had more black eyes, and bloody noses, and bruises than I care to remember. He was a mean, mean man. I don't remember a kind word from him. He beat most of us kids, but I got it the worst for some reason, and my mother, too. I'm telling you this because you have no idea the joy I have felt watching how your papa loved you and cared for you from the minute you were born. You had more love in one day from your papa than some people have in a lifetime with theirs. Me included. That love is still there in your heart, and it is not going anywhere.

You're going to lose him slowly. He will die from this, and it is going to be hard, maybe the hardest thing you will have to go through in your whole life, I don't know. But the love you two share is not going anywhere. It will stay with you forever. Meanwhile, honey, we can just take one day at a time, and one moment at a time, and sometimes even one breath at a time. But we will get through this. And yes, it won't be easy."

"I just miss him so much! And I know I'm lucky, he is the best papa ever, but now he is gone, and he doesn't know me anymore . . . I can't imagine that you had such a mean papa. But I know a boy at school who has black eyes a lot. He is probably beaten like you were. I know I'm lucky, but I don't feel lucky now."

"I know, sweetheart, I know," Margaret said as she rocked her daughter in her arms.

Margaret was not a crier, but almost every night now when she lay her head on the pillow, tears would well up, and she would allow herself to gently and quietly weep. She tried to hide her pain and be strong for Lena Bea by telling herself to pull up her socks and get on with it, that it could be worse. But no matter how many times she told herself to be strong and act like she had everything under control to other people, deep down she felt like a part of her was dying alongside her husband. She didn't know how to take her own advice.

The years seemed to drag on as Rene's health worsened. She would just get into a routine and think she had figured out how to handle the changes in him, but then a new symptom would appear. One minute he was going to the bathroom, the next day he was wetting himself. She would try and get him to change his pants, and he would just scream "No!" and she would have to struggle with him to get him changed. Sometimes she had to wait until he was asleep to change his clothes and slip a diaper on him.

Then there was the repeating stage where he would say the same thing over and over. Maybe a hundred times an hour. "So where do you live now?" was one that stuck for months. She was exhausted.

After the third year, Margaret sat down with Dr. Ingles and asked him for advice.

"I have been off work for almost two years, and I need to go back for financial reasons. But I'm so scared to leave him in someone else's care. And I want him to be at home as long as possible. But to be honest, Doc, I'm exhausted mentally and physically."

"Margaret, go back to work, it will do you good. I can arrange for a home care nurse to come to the house daily. They are trained and will do a good job caring for him. I think it is the best option. There is a cost, but I think the benefits will definitely outweigh that."

"I'll feel so guilty leaving him with someone else."

"I know, but you do need to care for yourself and your daughter. It will do you good to get back to work and out of the house. At least give it a try."

When she got home, she found Beatrice feeding Rene his lunch. She sat down at the table and started to cry. Her aunt came over and kissed her on the forehead.

"I really don't know how I could manage without you," Margaret said. "You have taken on so much since you got here. I'm sure you never imagined your retirement would mean looking after my husband, practically raising our child on your own, and looking after me! I feel like I have leaned on you so much since Rene got sick."

"Not another word. I'm so happy to be of some use, and you're my family. I wouldn't have it any other way," Beatrice said as she stroked her niece's back.

"I'm going to get help so I can go back to teaching. I'm trying to be strong, but I feel like I'm falling apart inside. I think going back to work might help. And we need the money."

"Take one day at a time, honey. I will be there to help you every step of the way." Auntie Beatrice reassured her. "Going back to work is a great idea;

it will do you good. And getting some help sounds perfect. You will know when the times comes, if it does, to put him in the hospital."

Sarah, age four and a half

"Why are you crying, Sarah?"

"I really miss my husband."

"Where is he?"

"He died. He was so sick, and I had to take care of him. He was so young when he died. It makes me so sad."

1958

Rene seemed to deteriorate quickly after the third year. He rarely spoke, and he had to be fed and bathed. He spent most of his time sitting in his wheelchair just looking off into space. In one way, it was easier to care for him, as it was more physical care he needed, but it was so sad to see his personality disappear before their eyes.

In the fourth year, the worst was when one day when he began to get agitated and fearful of sounds, any sound: a bird chirping or a car door closing would send him into a state of fear. Dr. Ingles explained it to her as a "fight or flight response." Whatever it was called, all she knew was that it took everything she had to calm him down. He would hold his breath and his narrow eyes would grow big and round. His body would stiffen up and an animal sound like "Heeee" would come out of his mouth as he sucked the air into his lungs. She could feel his heart racing as she held him and tried to comfort him. Then, in a voice which didn't even sound like his own, he would say, "wooo dar," which she finally figured out meant "Who's there?"

"It's just a bird, Rene, nothing to be afraid of," she would say in a calm, reassuring manner while stroking his head. But as the months went by, the fears became so frequent that she had to try everything to keep the house quiet.

She made up rules and posted signs around the house and on the front and back door. *Don't Knock When You Come In, No TV Allowed, No Radio Allowed, Don't Slam Drawers or Cupboards*. But it didn't help, and he got worse and worse. The fear in his eyes broke her heart. She finally asked Dr. Ingles for help.

C. INGRID DERINGER

"Dr. Ingles please, is there anything I can give him for his anxiety? He is now so fearful of sounds. I mean any sounds. I can't control a bird chirping, or a toilet flushing, or thunder booming," she said. "Is there any kind of pill you can give him?"

"I'm afraid nothing I know of seems to help. I'm so sorry. I have read some people say just plain chamomile tea, rose petal tincture, or verbena, which the Indigenous People around here use, is as good, if not better, than opioids."

Margaret left the office in a daze. "Tea? Is that really going to help?" she wondered.

She stopped at the store and bought chamomile tea and more adult diapers, and then asked the clerk where she might find rose petal tincture. The clerk looked at her with a puzzled look on her face, "I dunno."

When Dr. Ingles mentioned the local Indigenous remedies, it made Margaret think about her friend, Chief David White Raven.

The Big Buffalo Tribe near Millarville was familiar to her, as she and Rene had taken their science class to meet the chief and listen to his stories of the land, culture, and history of the area many times over the years. When she got home, she called the Chief without thinking about it twice.

"Can you bring him here, Margaret? Smiling Bear, our medicine man, can look at him and tell you what may help," he said.

"I don't know, Chief, he is so fearful. I'm afraid of taking him in the car all that way."

"Well, it would be better for him to come here if you can manage it."

"I'll make it happen."

Philip came from Calgary and helped Margaret lift Rene into the back seat of the car. Margaret sat beside him, and Philip drove to Big Buffalo Reserve. The trip was uneventful most of the time, maybe because Margaret and Philip sang to Rene the entire way—French songs, lullabies, and folk songs from his childhood. When they arrived, Philip lifted his older brother ever so gently into his wheelchair. Rene was calm until he heard a rooster, then he lost it, making the HEE sound and visibly shaking with fear.

Smiling Bear was there to greet them. Around his waist was a ceremonial cloth that was intricately beaded. Tucked into his beaded headband was a single eagle feather. He had jingles hanging around his ankles and suede moccasins. Margaret thought he looked regal with his braided hair and high cheek bones. He smiled at Rene with such a kind and tender expression that Margaret felt goose bumps on her arms. Smiling Bear gently touched Rene's hand and whispered something in his ear while he was in distress. Rene's face completely softened. It was a peaceful look that Margaret had not seen in over a year.

Smiling Bear then led them to a fire that was already aglow. They placed Rene on the ground on a blanket, and Margaret sat behind him for support. He was so frail and thin that Margaret could feel his ribs as she wrapped her arms around him and encouraged him to lean back into her frame.

Smiling Bear began to drum ever so softly, which only startled Rene a bit, but soon he began to sway along with the rhythm. The drum got faster and faster, and then suddenly stopped. Smiling Bear was silent, and Rene stopped swaying. They both looked to be in trance state from what Margaret could tell. They sat there for thirty minutes or more. Finally, Smiling Bear opened his eyes. He leaned over and touched Rene on the hand. Rene opened his eyes. He was staring into space but calm. A woman came over and the medicine man instructed her on what herbs to prepare.

"This is Singing Rabbit, she is my helper, and she will make a special tea for Rene," he told them.

Looking right at Margaret and Philip, he explained what he had discovered. "I have entered Rene's world and was with his spirit. Know that he is safe, and he is near to his crossing-over time. He has chosen this experience to learn and grow as a soul. And he tells me that everyone around him will also learn and grow from this. He had a special message for you, Margaret. He said not to worry, he will help you make sure your music will live on."

Margaret looked at Smiling Bear and could see his dark eyes sparkle. Almost as if he was still in a trance state.

"Understand that his illness was part of the master plan decided before he ever came to this earthly plane."

He paused, and then gently handed Margaret a cloth bag of medicinal herbs.

"These herbs will calm his transition. Give him this medicine twice a day until he passes."

Margaret and Philip took the bag and carried a very relaxed Rene back to the car. They sang every ballad they knew all the way home without an incident.

After the visit to the medicine man, Rene's fears seemed to vanish completely. Margaret would sing him to sleep every night, and when she bathed him, she would also sing to him. But he was deteriorating before her eyes. He rarely even uttered a sound now. He sat in his chair and looked out into nowhere. Margaret finally agreed with Dr. Ingles that it was time to put him in the long-term care ward of the hospital. She was afraid to lift him anymore. He weighed just under seventy pounds and was as fragile as a butterfly's wing. She was afraid to hurt him or drop him.

Every day after working at the school, she would go to the ward and spend time singing to him, and holding his hand, and telling him stories of their life together.

On January sixth, Margaret, Lena Bea, Aunt Bea, Jim, the neighbour boy who was like a son to Rene, and Philip all went together to the hospital to celebrate Rene's forty-second birthday. They had cake and balloons even though Rene was no longer responsive. As they sang "Happy Birthday," Lena Bea and Margaret held his hands and watched as a look of peace, almost a smile, came to his lips.

"I think he knows we are here," whispered Lena Bea, to which Margaret nodded.

Soon a nurse came in and took Margaret aside.

"He is near the end. It could be anytime now. I suggest you all say your goodbyes."

"Thank you, I'll tell them."

Margaret sat down and took Rene's hand. She noticed that each breath took longer and longer to come. Waiting for his next exhale, a slight moan seemed to come out, and then Margaret saw a faint, white, iridescent shimmering glow above his chest. It rose up into the ceiling. No inhale. He was gone.

It was a miracle to witness, and Margaret wasn't sure if anyone else had seen it, but it was an image that would stay with her till the day she herself died.

There were no tears. Margaret felt only a sense of relief as she drew a long breath and let out a sigh. She looked at Lena Bea and said, "He is gone, honey, he is gone."

Lena Bea covered her face with her hands. "Papa, Papa," she cried.

Jim put his arm around Lena Bea's shoulder and held her. Philip kissed his brother's head, and Aunt Bea stroked his head and said, "You're free now, sweetie, fly high. You're free."

When they came home from the hospital, Lena Bea ran upstairs to her bedroom, and Jim followed her. Margaret started to follow them.

"Just let her be, Margaret, Jim is with her," her aunt said. "She'll be okay."

Margaret sat at the kitchen table staring silently into space. Then she got up slowly and walked over to a drawer and took out a pair of scissors. With a stony look on her face, she went to the bathroom and locked the door.

She looked into the mirror, unwound her long braid from its bun, and without a thought or any expression on her face, she cut off her braid. It was the first time she had cut her hair in her entire life, but she showed no emotion as she looked at her reflection in the mirror. She took the braid and walked to the living room, then took the harmonica off the mantel and walked down the stairs to the basement. She pulled out the cedar chest that Rene built for them so long ago. It was where she kept their wedding outfits. As she opened the chest, she gently stroked the pressed flowers from their wedding day, her wedding dress, Rene's tweed suit and white shirt, and their wedding certificate. She then placed her braid on top, tucked the harmonica under the document, and closed the lid. She reached on the shelf for a pen and a label that she usually used for her canning jars.

She wrote *HARMONICA* in large letters and stuck the label on top of the cedar chest. She stood up, and then suddenly, she felt her legs go weak and she slumped to the floor. She dropped her head on the trunk and let out a wail that echoed throughout the house. From the depth of her being she began to sob. "How could you do this? We were supposed to grow old together. Lena Bea needs her papa. How could you have planned this? I don't understand."

Images played out in her head. She saw him in the yard, his goats following him around like a dog. She saw her neighbours and friends laughing at his silly jokes. She saw him showing the students on the science trips how to make a fire. She saw him making his goat soap with Lena Bea and Jim. She saw him kissing her for the first time on the stairs of Lily's Boarding House. She saw them dancing in the kitchen the first night they got their record player. She saw her own self holding his frail body against her as they sat near the fire and heard the rhythm of the drums.

One second, she was screaming with anger; the next, sobbing with grief; and finally, she was swearing. It was as if the five years' worth of tears and anguish that she had been holding back suddenly burst out from her chest like an explosion.

"God, if you really do exist then show me a sign because right now, I'm so damn angry with you for taking this kind, silly, sweet man away from all of us and making him suffer. What is the purpose of that? Why did you make him suffer? He didn't deserve that! Show me something. Explain it to me! Why?!" She screamed between sobs.

She sat there whimpering and holding her hand to her heart, rocking back and forth.

"Get up, Margaret. Get on with life and make the best of it, just like you always do. I'm more than fine. I'm free and whole. This was the plan."

It was Rene's voice in her head; it was as if he were there.

She could feel his hand rubbing her back ever so gently, like he often did just before they fell asleep at night.

"Rene, are you here?" she whispered with tears running down her cheeks.

The words of the medicine man came back to her. "It is part of his master plan that he chose before coming to this earthly plane."

"I'm here for you always," Margaret now heard. "I'll never leave you. Just think of me, and I'll be with you." Margaret sat on the floor, holding her breath and scanning the room, looking for Rene. She saw nothing.

Finally, she walked up the stairs. Beatrice was waiting with open arms.

1960

"Mom, wake up, you promised to take me to Lake Louise for the Junior trials. It's nine o'clock already," said fifteen-year-old Lena Bea.

Margaret was in a deep sleep and in the midst of a re-occurring nightmare of driving with her eyes closed. She was trying so hard to open her eyes, but they wouldn't open. She knew she was near a cliff and when her eyes finally opened, she was less than an inch from the cliff. Her daughter was in the back seat of the car, screaming, 'Mom, Mom Mommmmm.'"

Her eyes flew open, and her heart raced. "Mom! We gotta go!!!"

"What? What is it, Lena Bea?" she said groggily

"You promised to take me to Lake Louise, don't you remember?"

"Yes, of course, honey, give me a minute. What time is it?"

"It's nine o'clock. We have to leave in fifteen minutes to make it on time."

Margaret slid out of bed and got dressed. She brushed her teeth and washed her face and was in the car by nine fifteen.

"Mom, are you okay?"

"I'm fine, honey, I was just up late last night."

But, in fact, Margaret had been having trouble sleeping since Rene died two years earlier. She had recurring nightmares, always about driving the car with her eyes closed. Sometimes she was even in the back seat trying to steer the car. It always ended the same. She would try and try to open her eyes and when she finally did, she was on the edge of a mountainside, a second away from falling over the cliff.

"What does it mean?" she wondered. "I used to be fearless, and now I'm scared of everything. My ambition is gone. I'm fearful of trying anything new. I know it is ridiculous, but I can't stop the fear. Aunt Bea says it just is part of the grieving process and that it will pass. But it's been two years, and it is still bad, if not worse."

On her last visit to Calgary, she had popped in to see Mrs. Schmidt. They had a long talk.

"When my husband had his stroke at forty, I thought to myself, how am I going to manage? He was an engineer, bright, and very ambitious. We had money because he was involved in designing factory machines during the war. He was never out of work and thankfully, never had to fight in the war. We had a beautiful home and a healthy ten-year-old son. Life was great. Then, in one minute everything changed. Karl had a stroke that left him comatose for months. When he recovered from that, he had two more strokes. The whole time I couldn't sleep, couldn't eat. Everything is a blur really. I don't know how we got through it. Then one day maybe a year and a half later, I knew I had to smarten up for our son's sake. He was starting to act up in school, and the teacher called me in to say she was concerned. I knew I had to do something, if not for me, then for him. And although we had a lot of money saved up, I knew it wouldn't last forever.

So I learned how to fake it. I can't remember how I came up with the idea, but I just started pretending that I was in control and had the answers. I made decisions about moving and buying a boarding house without my husband's input, something I never would have done before. Karl was my rock. He was the decision maker. He did all the financial stuff. Me, I knew none of that. And now I had to take the reins, and I didn't have a clue. But I must say, it worked out. I honestly didn't know what I was doing, but I acted like I did. I'll never forget when I went to the bank manager and told him I was going to sell our home and buy a boarding house. He asked me all these money questions, and I just made-up numbers. Why he believed me, I'll never know. But I learned that if you show you're confident, even if you're not in the least, people believe you, and then eventually you believe you! I don't know if that helps you. But it is how I got through it. Pretty soon, I did get more confidence. Now look at me! I'm not rich, but I have made do over the years, and I can honestly say I have everything I need or want. My son is a successful businessman, and my husband managed pretty good till his death. I have my house and renters, lots of friends, and a grandchild on the way. I'm happy. What more does a person need?"

"Mrs. Schmidt, thank you. I feel like you're only one who understands what I have gone through and am still going through. I just feel out of control, and I think the recurring nightmares are about not having control. I learned at a young age to take control, get things done, move forward, but suddenly I don't even know where to start. All my hopes and dreams seem so unattainable. I can't even seem to decide what to eat or wear each day, let alone do a lesson plan for the children at school. I feel so bad for Lena Bea. I'm a terrible mother. I just feel so lost and so very tired!"

"Give it time. Time does heal. The old Margaret will return, and she will be stronger and even more confident."

"Time? It has been two years. How much longer will it take?"

"If you're here trying to figure this all out, my guess is, it will be soon. Start faking it, and you'll make it," she said as she took her hand and patted it.

"Now how about some nice kuchen and my good German coffee?"

When they got to Lake Louise, Margaret listened to her daughter's instructions.

"Come back in three hours. No parents are allowed to watch. Just go to the chalet restaurant, and I'll meet you there when I'm done. MOM! Are you even listening? MOM!"

Margaret had been daydreaming. "Yes? Where do I go?"

"Go to the chalet restaurant and sit down and wait for me. I'll meet you there. Oh, my God, Mom, do you even know where the restaurant is?" she said, rolling her eyes.

"Yes, I do, I'll go there now and wait," she said with a fake, weak smile. Lena Bea shrugged and let out a long sigh.

Margaret didn't even notice.

She went to the restaurant and sat near the fireplace. She ordered hot chocolate and a muffin, then picked up the newspaper on the side table and began to read the entertainment section. There was an advertisement that caught her eye.

Taking Submissions for Calgary Folk Festival.

Her eyes welled up with tears. "If it were years ago, I would have seen that ad and gone into gear trying to figure out how I could possibly get a submission to the festival. I was almost there. But that was the old Margaret. Those days are over. My dream is over. And that is okay. I don't have the drive or want any more anyway," she thought.

She pictured the cedar chest in her basement. Her dreams were laid to rest along with her harmonica, her wedding dress, and her hair. Sealed up forever. And in a way it was a comfort not to have to think about it anymore. The pressure she had always felt to succeed in the music industry was gone. It was sad but true.

"Fake it till you make it. Fake it till you make it." Mrs. Schmidt's words played over in her head. The only thing that she needed right now was to somehow get a feeling of being in control of her life, and perhaps Mrs. Schmidt had the answer.

BOOK TWO

Sarah, age three and a half

"When I was a mommy, I had a little girl. She had red hair."

"Red hair?"

"Yup, and I had red hair, too, down to my toes!"

"Holy smokes! That long?

"Yup, and I wore it in braids."

"Were you married when you were a mommy?"

"Yeah, he was a funny guy."

"Did you have lots of children?"

"No, just one girl with red hair. But she liked it short though, not long like me."

JIM
December 1979

Jim sat at his desk, sipping his coffee while he opened the mail. He had two reports yet to finish up from the night before: a stabbing incident at a party on Ragged Ass Road; and the drunk who missed a turn and drove into the ditch near Long Lake. Nothing too crazy considering it was a full moon.

A letter from RCMP headquarters listing the job postings caught his eye. *Turner Valley, Alberta.* His heart skipped a beat. He had spoken to the constables there a few times, and they seemed pretty content. It was a cushy job compared to Yellowknife. He had been thinking of applying for a transfer the last couple of years. He was tired of the freezing cold winters. And the job description sounded like he was a good fit. Without hesitation, he called headquarters and said he was interested. He knew he should talk to Patricia first, but he knew she would be totally against it, so he saw no point in even bothering to ask her.

Two days later, he got a call back.

"Jim, we have decided that with your background and advanced training with the drug unit, you would be the perfect choice for Turner Valley. Seems oil, money, and drugs go hand in hand," Constable Richards said.

"Great to hear. I accept," Jim said.

"The posting starts in three months. Does that work for your family?"

"Absolutely."

"All right, Jim, I'll send the paperwork for you to sign. Should be there in a few days. Congratulations."

"Pat, I got a new assignment today."

"Oh, yeah. What is it?"

"It's in Turner Valley, Alberta. It's a ten-minute drive from Millarville."

"I don't think so."

"Patricia, Mom is battling breast cancer, I would like to be with her. I wasn't there for my dad. And Mom already transferred the deed for the acreage to me. We could tear down the old house and build a new one. There is so much more opportunity for the boys there, too. And it's a promotion. A lot more investigative work, which I like."

"I don't want to leave my family, Jim. I've never lived anywhere else. You know that."

"Look, you're not the one who has to spend so much time outside fighting the bitter cold and the crazy wind, working in the dark all winter long, having to take snowmobiles into remote areas to deal with accidents and domestic violence. Not to mention having horse flies and mosquitoes the size of small birds eat you alive all summer. Those buggers love me. You're indoors most of the time. You don't have to fight the elements."

He really wanted to bring up the fact that she had a pretty cushy life, but he held back. When they got married, Pat quit her secretarial job right away, without even discussing it with him. She just presumed that she didn't have to work anymore he guessed. She was indoors most of the time, watching copious amounts of television and visiting her friends and family. She was a good mother to the boys though, and she did keep the house in order, so he didn't feel he could complain too much.

"It is too late anyway. I accepted the position, and I report to work in three months," he said and walked out of the room.

IF I COULD LIVE AGAIN

Three months later—March 9, 1980

Jim woke to the smell of a chinook. The chinook winds that brought summer to Millarville—just when you had enough with the cold winter days—was one thing Jim had missed when he moved away to Yellowknife after graduating from the RCMP Academy. The familiar warm, earthy smell that made you want to go for a picnic, or go fishing, or sit outside on a lawn chair with a beer and have a barbeque was wonderful. Some people complained of headaches when the winds arrived, but for him chinooks made him feel renewed. And he needed it. It had been stressful the last few months. Patricia was so miserable and negative and was barely speaking to him. Her words echoed in his head: "You tricked me. You never even asked me what I wanted before you accepted the job. Do you think I'm stupid?"

He knew she would react that way, and that was why he never asked her. He needed the change, or he was going to go crazy. He was fed up with Yellowknife, and if he were honest, it wasn't just the climate. He wanted to go back home, especially once his mom had gotten sick. He was all she had. She had begged him to come home. And he didn't ever feel he belonged in Yellowknife. Anyway, his mind was made up. And he hated to admit it, but if he didn't have his sons, he would have easily left Patricia behind. He often wondered if he ever loved her or had just married her on the rebound from Lena Bea. His mother had said as much, not in those exact words of course, but she alluded to it when he was home for his dad's funeral. Patricia didn't want to come, saying she didn't know the man so why should she go to his funeral. His mother was not a judgmental person in the least. He never remembered her saying anything bad about anyone ever. But when Patricia didn't show up, she was hurt.

"There is something not right with that girl, Jim. I hate to say it, but not coming to her own father-in-law's funeral to support you is just not right. Are you two having problems? Perhaps you married too quickly, son. It's just not right. Not right at all."

But it was his first chinook since coming back, and he didn't want to dwell on all the drama going on with him and Pat, hashing out in his mind all the problems they were having. His thoughts turned to Margaret. Ever since moving back, he had fallen into his old routine of spending time at the farmhouse. Her place felt more like home than his own house. It had been that way since he was a little boy. He had Rene to thank for his upbringing. His own father was so severely depressed that he often wondered how his life would have turned out if he hadn't had Rene in his life. He showed him how to fix things and repair everything from broken fences to toasters. He taught him how to drive and repair the little 1941 Massey tractor they used to pull the swather when they cut hay. He was the one who taught him how to fish, and ride a bike, and hit a baseball. He could still recall when Rene took him aside one day shortly after he was diagnosed.

"Son, I don't know how this dementia thing is going to pan out, nor how quickly I'll deteriorate, and so I want to talk to you man to man before it gets too bad. Now this is between the two of us. Understand?"

"Yes, of course I understand. Just between us."

He remembered standing there in the barn, having just turned twelve the week before.

He was only an inch shorter than Rene, but whereas Rene was a stocky, strong and muscular man, he was lanky and thin.

"You have been the son I never had. I want you to have my tool belt and all my tools. I know I have taught you a lot about fixing things, but there is more I can still teach you. Now if I act strange, it's because I see things I'm not supposed to see, but they are real to me, as real as you standing here. Don't be frightened. And if I stare off into space, just wait a bit, I'll come back. Now, I need you to be the man around here. Look after my girls. They will need a good man like you. I've watched you grow into a responsible young man with a heart bigger than Prince Edward Island. I know you have responsibilities at home, too, but I think you can handle it. Just do your best. That is all I ask. So from now on, till I'm no-good-for-nothing, I want us to spend time together so I can teach you more about fixing and all the things that need to be done to run our little farm. Everything I'll teach you will come in handy your whole life. Margaret calls them "life skills" and says people don't learn this stuff in school. I have a knack for fixing that my pa would say is a gift. My brother never had that knack, and neither did my pa. But you do, I see that in you as clear as the nose on your face. It's a way of seeing things that other people just don't see."

Jim still remembered holding back the grief he felt in that moment with everything he had, and how he knew that if he let himself cry, his world would have shattered into a million pieces.

"I promise to look after your girls, Rene, and I really appreciate you teaching me everything you know."

"We got a deal then?"

"Yes."

"Then let's shake on it, Son."

But Jim remembered looking at Rene's outstretched hand and how he disregarded it, wrapping his arms around him in a bear hug instead.

He could still remember the long, warm embrace, the feeling of Rene's strong arms around him, and hearing him sniffle and his voice crackle just a bit when he comforted him. "It's going to be okay, Son. We'll get through this one way or another." It was a tender moment, one that was embedded in his mind.

As Rene's health slowly worsened, Jim had taken over the chores and the caring of the acreage. He was sixteen when Rene died. Margaret had taught him to drive the car, and she let him use it anytime she didn't need it. Margaret went into a depression, not like his father had done though. She didn't drink, and swear, and cry; she just hardly spoke. He never heard her laugh, or sing, or hum songs, or play her guitar. She didn't bake or make pickles or bread like she used to. She just seemed to sit in the window in her rocking chair and stare out the window. He was glad he knew what to do to keep things running. He and Lena Bea—or BB as he called her—kept up the milking and goat soap making. He plowed up the garden, then he and Aunt Bea planted and cared for it. Jim's own mom even learned how to make pickles with Aunt Bea's help, though they never tasted like Margaret's, not that he ever said anything. He wasn't sure if Margaret even noticed all the things that he, BB, and Aunt Bea did during those years. The house was so filled with grief that you could cut it with a knife. It was in that time that he and BB got closer and closer, and they began to fall in love.

Jim decided to go over to Margaret's and have his morning coffee with her. As he walked into the yard, he saw her hanging out her laundry on the clothes line. "Typical Margaret!" he said to himself and smiled. "Hanging out clothes the minute the weather is nice even though she has a perfectly good dryer."

He got closer and realized that the clothes on the line were Rene's. He stopped and stared. He remembered Rene's clothing, the small white T-shirts that he always wore, his dark brown trousers, and the grey pullover sweater that he lived in.

"Dear God," he thought, "Rene has been dead for over twenty years, and she still has his clothing?" He ducked behind a tree and stood still, not knowing if he should go home and pretend that he never saw her hanging out her dead husband's clothes, or if he should go and ask her what the heck she was doing? He decided on the latter.

"Margaret, good morning!"

"Jim, my favourite man. How are you on this beautiful day?"

"Aw, couldn't be better. Nothing like a chinook on your day off."

"A glorious day, yes, it is," she said as she continued hanging up the last of the clothing from her basket. "How about a nice cup of coffee? I just made it. We can sit on the porch."

"Sounds perfect."

As they sat on the porch, Jim finally got up the nerve up to ask her about Rene's clothing. As a police officer he was taught that the best way to bring up a delicate subject was just to state the obvious, and then see how they responded.

"I see you're hanging up Rene's clothing on the line," he said.

"Yes, I like to do that every spring so they don't get all dusty."

"Margaret, why on earth do you still have his clothing in your closet after twenty years?"

"Oh, I just can't seem to get rid of them. Seeing them in the closet and in the drawers gives me comfort somehow."

"Yes, but don't you want to move on? You are still young and healthy, and dare I say, as beautiful as ever."

"Oh, it is good to have you back! I see you haven't lost your charm! Sixty-three is hardly young. And if you're suggesting I go out and find myself a man, forget it. No man could compare to Rene, and I would be doing just that, comparing every man I met to him. No siree, I'm quite content with my life, Jim. Don't you worry one bit about me. Now tell me, how are those two strapping boys of yours doing since moving here? Do they like it?"

"They are fitting in just fine. Pat is taking them back to Yellowknife in a few weeks to go to a cousin's wedding. I want to stay behind because of Mom. She is nearing the end now."

"Yes, I saw her yesterday, poor thing. I brought her some of her favourite cookies. You know the ones with dates in the middle? But she hardly had a bite. She did smile though."

Later, as Jim was barbequing hamburgers for supper, he began to think about whether to call BB and tell her about her mother hanging Rene's clothing on the line. He hadn't called her since moving back. He had kept up with BB's life through his weekly phone calls to Margaret, not that he needed to be updated. She was in the news a lot. Her professional skiing career, her retirement after her fall in the Innsbruck Olympics, and then her fundraising endeavours, and of course, the commercials of her on the TV with her sports clothing line and her "Super Ski Wax." It was just too hard to pick up the phone and talk to her. When he saw her at his dad's funeral five years before, it was torture not to go and wrap his arms around her and hold her. "God, how I miss that woman," he thought. "Will I ever get over her? Even though she dumped me for Robert, Mr. Hunk with the connections and rich daddy?"

He still loved her, even though she had left him completely and utterly devasted and broken-hearted. He couldn't help it. He didn't blame her. His buddies warned him all through high school that she was way out of his league, but he didn't want to believe it. They were in love. But deep down, he always knew she was destined to be someone great, and he was destined to be a small-town boy. And that is exactly how their lives played out.

Besides, he thought, it really was not his business if Margaret kept her dead husband's clothes in her closet. It probably happened more than people realized. Perhaps not for over twenty years, but nevertheless, it wasn't doing any real harm. Margaret seemed to be doing great. She still subbed at the school. She had her little acreage and garden, was active in the community, and seemed more content than ever. And she had definitely softened up in her old age. She seemed less serious and driven. He had noticed that she was a night hawk though. Often times when he was coming back from a call in the middle of the night, he would see her lights on and her silhouette in the window by her writing desk.

Jim hadn't asked her about it, probably because he was a night hawk, too. He hadn't always been like that. But in the last five or so years, it was like he had discovered the peacefulness of the nighttime. It was the quiet he loved. Patricia was a talker. She talked constantly, about nothing mostly. It was like she was afraid of a pause. If he didn't answer her quickly when she was firing questions, she would start nagging that he never listened, or that he didn't care about her. When he first met her, he had thought she was a cute little chatterbox, but now it was just plain exhausting listening to her. The more she talked over the years, the less he talked, and the more he worked and stayed up late to avoid her. He knew it was wrong. She was his wife. But it seemed they were growing apart on so many levels.

July 3, 1992

It was eight in the morning, and Jim didn't have to be at work till ten. He had his uniform in a bag to take to work. He wanted to run over to Margaret's to do a couple of things before he headed out. He was eating his cereal and reading the newspaper at the same time, when he heard Patricia in the living room whispering to someone. His ears perked up.

"I gotta go, I'll see in a few days... I do, too. Yup, okay, bye."

Patricia walked into the kitchen and poured herself a cup of coffee.

"Going somewhere?"

"Ah, yes. I was going to tell you. I'm going home for a while."

"Again? What is it this time? You've been back four times in the last year."

"Oh, you know, it's Mom. She's just feeling lonely since Dad died. Why do you care anyway? You're always working or over at Margaret's, and even when you are home, you don't talk to me anyway. The kids don't need me anymore. Why shouldn't I go home when I want?"

"I'm not saying you shouldn't. I was just asking if you were going somewhere in particular."

"The kids are gone, living their lives in the big city. I'm utterly bored. I have no friends."

"I know."

"You have no idea," she yelled as she stormed up the stairs.

He heard her getting the suitcases out of the closet and swearing to beat the band. "Fucking asshole. God damn it. Where's that fucking makeup bag. Jesus Christ…"

He got up from the table. "I gotta get out of here," he thought. He left his cereal half eaten and went into the garage to search for his tool belt.

"Shit, I swear I hung it up here." He looked around. "Damn it, woman, where did you put it?" he said under his breath. "She's always moving my stuff around. God damn it." He finally eyed it in the corner on the floor. He knew he had not left it there.

He drove to Margaret's. He grabbed his tool belt from the passenger seat and walked up to the house. He knocked lightly at the front door and walked in.

"Morning!" he yelled.

No answer. The coffee pot was on the stove. Buns were rising on the counter.

"Margaret?"

He went to the back door. She was on the ground, twisted round with one foot still stuck in a broken step. Her head was in a pool of blood, and blood covered the metal pole that was holding up the clothes line. The clothes basket was turned over. Laundry was scattered in the dirt.

"Margaret!" He touched her face. "Margaret, are you alright?"

She moaned and tried to speak. Her mouth seemed drooped.

"You're going to be okay. I'm going to call the ambulance."

He ran into the house and picked up the phone.

"Gerry, Jim Heart here. Margaret Gallant fell and has a head injury and possible stroke. I'm with her in the back."

"We are on our way, Jim."

He held her hand. "Margaret, I'm here. Hang in there. Help is on its way," he said as he pressed a towel to her head with his other hand.

She was trying hard to speak, but it was difficult to make out what she was saying. He leaned close to her mouth.

"Dresser," she said.

"Did you say 'dresser,' Margaret?"

"Yee."

"Okay, Margaret. Rest. Everything is going to be okay." But he knew even as he said it that she was slipping away. He had seen it enough times in his career. But seeing Margaret, who had been like a mother to him, made it different. He was not the calm collected witness to death as he had been many times in his life as a police officer. Instead, he felt panic and fear.

"Margaret, please, please stay with me," he said as the tears rolled down his face. Just then Gerry showed up. He pulled Jim away. "Jim, I need you to move."

Jim was blabbering, "Five minutes sooner. Oh, God, how could I have let this happen, BB, Rene… I'm so sorry. I should have fixed that step."

"Jim, this is not your fault, man. She fell. It was an accident. Come on, let's go," Gerry said as he pushed him into the back of the ambulance.

Doc Lafontaine placed his hand on Jim's shoulder. "She's gone, Jim. I'm so sorry. There was nothing I could do. My guess is that she had a stroke when she fell. The injury is what killed her, I think, but an autopsy would determine the cause for sure if that's what the family wants. Do you want to call Lena Bea? I know you are friends. Or I can call her if you prefer."

Jim tried his best to be professional, but as he shook Doc's hand, his legs went weak and he felt faint.

"Jim, sit down, are you alright? Gerry, get him some water. Put your head between your legs. That a boy. You're okay, you're going to be okay."

After a few moments, Jim raised his head and looked at Doc. "I want to call BB."

"Okay, Jim. Just take some time to compose yourself."

"BB, it's Jim here."

"Jim, what a nice surprise! How are you? Haven't talked since the Ma's seventy-fifth birthday party."

"BB, I'm calling in an official capacity, I'm afraid your mom passed away today."

"Mom? Are you sure?"

"Yes, I'm sure. It looks like it was a freak accident. She was hanging her laundry out when the step gave way. Her foot went through and got stuck, and she hit her head on the corner of the metal pole of the clothes line. It also looks like she may have had a stroke at the same time. They're not sure. I found her. I went over to do a few little repairs for her before heading off to work and when I got there, I found her on the ground. She was barely conscious. Gerry and Bob came with the ambulance, but Doc Lafontaine said she passed away within a few minutes of arriving."

"But that can't be."

As a police officer, Jim was used to that typical response. He just had to continue to explain. It would sink in eventually.

"Is Robert home?"

"No, he's away on a buying trip."

"I'm going to come over BB. I'll be there in half an hour. I can bring you back here."

"Oh, my God, Jim! Ma is dead? But… I don't understand I just… She fell? Did she suffer?"

Jim could tell by her voice that it was starting to register. "No, it happened quite fast. She may have had a headache, but I doubt she suffered. From what I could tell, it happened just before I arrived."

Jim made the part up about not suffering. He had no idea if she did or not. Should he tell her he meant to repair the step? That it was on his list of things to do, but he never got around to it? No. He couldn't.

"I'm going to hang up now. I'll be there soon, BB. Call Robert and get someone to look after the kids when they get home from school. Do you have a neighbour or someone close by?"

On the drive to Calgary, Jim thought about BB. Whenever he did that, he relived the scene at the Post Hotel in Lake Louise, a scene that had haunted him for the last twenty-eight years. It was like a bad movie that he played over and over.

"She's at the Post Pub. I'm sure she went there after work," a young woman told him when he asked at her dorm. He was there to surprise her. He walked into the Post Pub and there she was sitting with a man, deep in conversation. The man was holding her hand.

The band was playing in the background, and people were slow dancing on the dance floor. The room was dark, and he could still remember how the smell of beer and cigarettes filled the air. She had the look Jim knew all too well, one that he thought was only reserved for him. But there it was. That sweet turned-up mouth, the intent look in her emerald green eyes. Her cheeks, sun kissed from skiing. She was so beautiful. She was leaning forward, hanging on to this guy's every word. She looked up when she heard Jim's voice.

"BB?"

She jumped at the sight of him, and then stood up and rubbed her hands on her jeans. Her face turned red. The shamed look she wore was one he would never erase from his memory. One glance at the guy sitting there and he got it. He was a hunk: square jaw, blonde hair, piercing blue eyes, and muscles bulging out of his t-shirt. He was someone you would see on the cover of a *Sports Illustrated* magazine or in a commercial.

Like an idiot, he sat down and listened to the guy—who clearly did not know who Jim was—go on and on about how great Lena was and how he was going to set up a meeting with his dad's friend, who was Nancy Green's coach. After twenty minutes of torture, Jim got up and said he had to go meet someone. BB looked at him. A tear rolled down her cheek. It was in that moment that he knew it was over. This Robert guy was in her league. His buddies were right. What did he have to offer her? Nothing except a boring life in some rural community.

When BB opened the door of the penthouse, Jim caught his breath. She was dressed in white linen pants, a blue silk top, and high heels. Her hair was in a pixie cut, and she had on black-rimmed round glasses. She looked much like the picture he had just seen of her in the lifestyle section of *The Calgary Herald* the week before for some benefit she was hosting. She was stunning, even with her red, puffy eyes. He wondered how she could look that good that early in the day, never mind that she had just found out her mother died?

"Jim, thank you so much for coming. I don't think I'm fit to drive."

She almost fell as she reached for the door handle. He caught her and held her in his arms till he felt her body gain some control. He looked past her into her penthouse, at the wall of windows, the modern white-leather furniture, and large wall-art and carvings. It was wealth beyond anything he had ever seen. It was enough for him to realize his fantasy was just that. "She's out of your league, pal." His grade eight friend's voice drove the all-too familiar wedge into his hopes. But for the life of him, even now in this time of grief, he could not erase the image of the two them married and growing old together.

He drove her to Millarville to see her aunt, and then later to the hospital. After dropping her back at home, Jim walked back to his car and sat for a moment. "What in the Sam hell is the matter with you, man? She is a happily married woman, and she is vulnerable right now. Her mother just died. Get a grip on yourself. Get her out of your mind," he told himself. But he couldn't. He could still smell her scent on his jacket, and it was intoxicating. The last time he had held her that close was at his father's funeral, and he still wasn't over that feeling, even after five years.

BOOK THREE

Sarah, age five

"*What are you painting?*"

"*It's my family. This is my auntie. This is my husband. This is me, and this is my daughter.*"

"*Who's the boy by the fence?*"

"*Oh, that's my son who lives next door. He helps making goat soap.*"

"*Goat soap? What do you do with the goat soap?*"

"*We sell it, of course. I like the one with lavender in it. But I don't like milking the goats.*"

"*Do you sell anything else?*

"*Garlic and vegetables, and sometimes my bread and pickles.*"

LENA BEA
July 3, 1992

Lena Bea sat in her lounge chair on the deck of her Calgary penthouse that overlooked the Bow River. She was re-reading Louis Hay's book *You Can Heal Yourself* and sipping a cup of jasmine tea. Natalie Cole was singing "Unforgettable" in the background on the radio when the phone rang. She picked up her cell phone. "Hello, Auntie Bea," Lena Bea said. "How are you doing today? Still in pain?"

"Never mind my darn hip, where's your mother? I know something is wrong. She never came to see me today, and she isn't answering the phone, and I had a dream, or it seemed like one anyway. She was standing at the foot of my bed, smiling at me, and she said, 'It's time to go home now.' It was so real. And then she never showed up."

"Whoa, slow down, Auntie. I'm sure everything is fine. I'll call Jim and Patricia to go take a look, and I'll call you back. Don't worry, honey. I'm sure she is just off doing something."

She had never heard her Aunt Bea so stressed out. She was always so sweet on the phone.

No sooner had she hung up the phone when it rang again. "BB, it's Jim here."

Lena Bea put the phone down softly. "Ma! No!" she said out loud. She heard her heart pounding and felt a wave of electricity rise from her toes up into her throat. She screamed.

"Ma. No, you can't leave me! Ma. Oh, Ma…"

Suddenly it hit her that Aunt Bea must have had a vision of her mom as she passed. She was right. Oh, God, she had to tell Aunt Bea in person. She would be devastated. And the kids. "Oh, God, Alex will be traumatized," she thought.

She got up off the floor and called Robert, but there was no answer.

As she waited for Jim, she thought about her Aunt Bea. She was 103 years old but looked and acted like a seventy-five-year-old. She was only in the seniors' level four care unit because she had broken her hip at her weekly square-dancing class so she wasn't able to manage on her own, and Ma's place had stairs.

"Oh, God, she will be a mess when I tell her," she thought.

She called her neighbour, who was a good friend.

"Mary-Ann, I just had a call that my mom died."

"Oh, Lena, I'm so sorry.

"She had a fall and hit her head. I'm going to Millarville with a friend. I may be back in time, but just to be safe, can you come over for the kids? They get off the bus at four."

"Yes, of course I will. Don't worry about a thing. I'll just tell the kids you had to make a run to Millarville. You can talk to them when you return."

"You still have a spare key?"

"Yes, I do. Don't worry, I'll look after the kids. Take your time."

As Lena Bea hung up, there was a buzz at the front door. "Jim, is that you?" she said through the intercom.

"Yes, BB, I'm here."

"Come on up to the penthouse."

When she opened the door and saw Jim in his uniform her heart sank, and her body felt near to collapse. She leaned on the door handle to steady herself. He grabbed her just before she fell. He held her and hugged her, and as he did, he kept repeating, "It's okay, BB, I'm here. Let it out."

She sobbed into his shoulder as he rubbed her back.

As they drove to Millarville, Lean Bea talked.

"It's so surreal. Mom was rarely sick. She never took any pills or even vitamins. Well, you know as well as I do, she was as healthy as a horse. But you said she might have had a stroke?"

"Yes, it seemed that she did."

"So ironic. The first time she went to a hospital was also her last. Even when she had me it was a home birth that went without a hitch. Mom was very proud of the fact that the only time she was ever in a hospital was to visit."

"She was a tough cookie, your mom, there's no doubt about that! She was one of a kind and I'll tell you, the whole community is going to miss her big time. She was well loved and respected."

"Yes, she was, wasn't she? God, I can't believe I'm using the past tense. I just can't believe she is gone. My little Alex will be heartbroken. He adored her and followed her around like he was stuck to her. Mom used to say that he was like a wood tick, and then she'd laugh like crazy. She had a special way with him. Well, you know Alex and his million questions, eh? Mom said he never got out of the "why" stage that three-year-old children are famous for. Of course, she loved that inquisitive mind and she never tired of his questions. In fact, she encouraged them."

"Yes, Alex and his grandmother were quite the pair."

Lena stayed quiet the rest of the trip, looking out the window with tears streaming nonstop down her face. He handed her a clean, white hankie from the inside pocket of his uniform.

"Oh, Jim, only you would have a hankie. You're so sweet." She sobbed even louder.

When she got to Aunt Bea's room, she didn't need to tell her anything. Aunt Bea knew as soon as she saw her face.

"I knew it!" Aunt Bea stated. "She stood there right at the end of bed and said it was time to go home. It was so clear. What do you think she meant by home?"

"I don't know, Auntie. We may have to die before we find that out."

But Lena Bea did know. She had had a near-death experience, an experience she had never shared with anyone because she doubted anyone would believe her, but it was as vivid today as it was the day it had happened. It was after the avalanche accident when she was buried in snow on the ski hill. She knew where her mom had gone, and it was the most amazing place, where love and beauty could never be compared to anything on this earth. The colours were so vibrant, and with an iridescent yellow hue that permeated everything. She had never seen the like before or since. She had seen her life pass before her eyes from birth to the present. "It was as real as standing here," she thought. "More real, in fact." Then she was met by her father, and he told her that her time was not up yet and that she would be going back. He reassured her that she would heal from her accident, and she knew it was true. She saw her future, and she was well. In an instant she felt a pull and was back in her body, but in the hospital intensive care.

She had opened her eyes and a nurse had said, "You came back! We'd thought we'd lost you for good. You're very brave. You're going to be all right."

It took a few weeks to really comprehend the whole experience. And afterwards, she never feared death again.

She knew her mom had experienced that same thing when she passed. She had read enough about near-death experiences to know it was a universal phenomenon. As she thought about it, she began to feel calmer knowing her mom was in a beautiful place, where the most intense feeling of love existed and that she would be reunited with her husband. "Home, yes, home," she thought with a slight smile.

"I never thought she would go before me. Never. Well, now it's my turn, and hopefully I won't have to wait too long." Beatrice sobbed.

At that moment, when Lena Bea looked at her great aunt, she saw her frailness for the first time. Why had she never noticed it before? She had always seemed to be so strong and sure of herself. It was like Lena Bea was seeing her aunt in a new light. She was thin; her plump, round face was gone. In its place was a face with sunken cheeks and saggy bags under blood-shot eyes.

Lena Bea encouraged her aunt to lie down. She sat beside her bed and held her hand for what seemed an hour till she drifted off to sleep.

Jim was waiting for her in the hall.

"I can't believe you're still here, Jim. Thank you!"

He smiled. "Of course, I am. Do you want to see your mom?"

"Yes, please."

Except for a gash that was stitched up and a bruise on her left temple, it looked like her mom was just sleeping. Lena Bea touched her just to make sure she was truly dead. Her hand was cold and lifeless. She looked at her body and could see the life was gone; her spirit was gone; her mom was gone.

"She's not here, Jim."

"I know BB." He placed his hand gently on her shoulder.

They drove back to Calgary and remained silent the whole time. Lena Bea watched the scenery out the window, remembering the stories her mom told her about coming to Calgary, and her first trip to Millarville, and how she loved the countryside the minute she saw it. As she watched the farms pass by, the smell of fresh-cut hay filled her nostrils. Her mother always said that the smell of fresh-cut hay was her favourite. In the car mirror she saw the snow-capped mountains. The beauty took her breath away. It was the first time she really understood what it was about this countryside that her mother loved so much.

Jim parked the car, then got out and went around to the passenger side to open the door for her. She was staring into space.

"BB, we're here."

He gently took her hand and walked with her up to her penthouse door. She looked up at him and touched his face.

"I don't know how to thank you. You're a true friend."

She put her hand on the doorknob, and then hesitated and looked back at him. "You have been so amazing today. I forgot what a sweet man you are." She leaned in and gently kissed his cheek, smiled, and walked inside.

Alex was waiting for her. At eleven years old, he was already tall for his age. She was always so shocked at how handsome he was becoming. His eyes were baby-blue, his hair was dark brown and curly, and it hung in natural ringlets so it was much longer than it looked. It was thick and bounced when he walked. He was already five foot seven and had size ten feet. He was physically very strong and muscular. He wore his height well. He had never gone through the awkward or clumsy stage like many young people did. He was a confident young boy and so eager to help people. As well, his sense of humour was a gift for her that balanced out her seriousness.

"What's up, Mom? MaryAnn said you had to run to Millarville at the last moment. Is everything okay with Grandma?"

MaryAnn looked at Lena Bea, motioned that she was leaving, then gave her an empathic look and put her hands together in a praying position. As she left, she blew her a kiss and touched her heart.

"Let's sit down, honey." She took his hand and walked him over to the couch where they sat down.

"Your grandma died today. She fell and hit her head and she died. She didn't suffer. It was all very quick."

"No!" Alex shouted and stood up.

"Yes, honey, I'm so sorry."

"Nooooo!" Alex screamed.

He ran into his bedroom and slammed the door. Lena Bea let him go. She sat on the couch listening to his sobbing and shouting. She decided she would wait till he calmed down a bit before going to him. She hated to admit it, but the close bond he had with her mom had made her jealous sometimes. She never had that closeness with her own mom. She was the apple of her papa's eye and everyone knew it. God, how she missed him even after all these years. Images of her screaming at her mother came flooding back. Too many times, she hated to admit, she had told her that she wished she were the one who died instead of her papa because at least he cared about her. She looked up, "Ma, I'm so sorry for all those times I said that." Tears rolled down her face. "I'm so sorry."

Sandy came into the living room. She was five years old, the smallest in her class but smart as a whip. She was the creative one in the family and the spitting image of Robert—baby-blue eyes and straight blonde hair. She had been playing in her room and talking to herself as usual. It sounded like she was playing "store," her favourite game. She may have looked like Robert but she was a mama's girl through and through.

"Why is Alex crying, Mommy? Mommy! You're crying. What's wrong?"

"Come sit down, honey, I have something I need to tell you."

Three weeks after her mom's death, Lena Bea decided it was time to finish packing up the last of her parent's belongings from the farmhouse and spending some time with Aunt Beatrice who was near the end, according to the doctors. She asked MaryAnn to keep the children for the weekend, and she happily agreed. She kissed them goodnight and headed out, hoping to get an early start in the morning.

As she drove, the sun was setting, the skies were purple and pink, and the air was still. She had the top down on her new Mercedes Convertible 500SL, and a green silk scarf of her mother's tied at the chin. She felt like she was driving into a dream. A hint of guilt came over her for leaving the children behind, but she needed the quiet to go through the personal belongings. She knew her mother saved everything, but she had no idea just how much stuff she actually had in that small farm. It was a testament to her mother's pack rat tendencies as to why Lena Bea was a minimalist.

She woke up in the morning thinking that today the tears would stop. It seemed like she had been crying for three weeks straight. As she looked in the bathroom mirror, she noticed that her bright green eyes looked dull and bloodshot. Her short, wavy red hair looked like that of a rooster. She needed a haircut and her nails done before the funeral.

"God, stand up straight, you're stooped over like an old woman!" She told her reflection in the mirror. "You look like the last rose of summer."

She jumped into the shower and used her mother's shampoo. It was her homemade shampoo that she made with lavender and rosemary. As she toweled off, she looked into the mirror. She had her mother's face and hair colour and the god-awful curls that drove her crazy. Unlike her mother though, who wore her hair long and always in a bun or a braid, she kept her hair short and got it styled on a regular basis. She did this, not so much to be up-to-date with the times, but because she was so bad at styling it herself. It was a struggle to get it to look decent. She thought of letting it grow so many times, but she just didn't have the patience to wait out the ugly phase of letting the layers grow out.

She dragged the boxes her mother had stored in the closets, the base-ment, and the upstairs back room and piled them into the living room, then plopped herself down on the floor. Every photo, every pottery bowl her mom had ever made, every card, every piece of jewelry, every LP from her parent's record collection brought on the waterworks. It wasn't just the memories, she realized, it was having to deal with everything herself. Robert couldn't be there to help her because he was mostly out of town this time of year on buying trips for the clothing line. Aunt Beatrice would have been the perfect person to help her, but when she popped in to see her, she wasn't even responding anymore. The nurses told her she was shutting down physically and mentally and that they didn't expect she would last more than a few weeks. Her mom's friends and her uncle were all too old to be of much help. It was ironic because her mom had always been there for her, taking care of everything, and helping her out after her big accident and after Sandy was born. Now it was her turn to take care of her mother in a way. And she was not good at it. She could hear her mom's voice in her head yelling at her to clean up her room. "Pull up your bootstraps and get on with it. Start in one corner and work your way around. One thing at a time, Lena Bea, it is not that hard!" Which was funny when she thought of it because her mother *never* did one thing at a time. She did ten things all at once, that is, when she finally got over her depression. She would be making wine, cutting vegetables for dinner, doing laundry, and have bread rising on the counter, all while organizing a fundraiser on the telephone. She remembered feeling tired just watching her.

If it were possible to hire someone to clean up the farm, she would have done it. But she knew she had to do it herself. She needed to go through everything, relive the memories, and yes, perhaps keep some things, if not for herself, then at least for the children.

"Come on in!" she yelled from the living room when she heard the knock.

"Hello? BB?"

"I'm in here."

She was sitting on the floor with boxes surrounding her, sorting jewelry and pictures and knick-knacks. Her mother was always about supporting local art and crafts, and she had so much stuff. It was incredible. All over the house there were doilies, knitted shawls, croqueted toilet paper holders, carvings, pictures, even a fake bird's nest stuck on what looked like a piece of driftwood with a clock attached. And the Christmas ornaments! There were some real doosies. Many were ones her students had made emblazoned with the words: *Best Teacher, I Love you Mrs. Gallant, Favourite Teacher.* Then, of course, there was every single card her students ever gave her and every sympathy card from her papa's funeral. "Stuff!!!" She thought.

"Hi BB, seems you have your job cut out for you!"

"Jim, what a surprise! Oh my God, you have no idea!"

"I have the weekend off, give me a job. I'm here to help."

"Oh, Jim, you shouldn't have! But, boy, I would be crazy to say no. I'm so overwhelmed. And to be honest, you're the only person I would feel comfortable going through all this stuff with."

"Great, Pat went to Yellowknife for a visit, and I'm actually not on duty this weekend so I'm all yours."

They spent the day sorting and hauling things to the dump. As they worked, they chatted away about everything—her mom, Rene, growing up, the goats, their kids, and Millarville.

It was late in the day by the time Lena Bea decided to finally show Jim what she had found in the bedroom.

"I have something I need to show you."

She took his hand and led him into her mother's closet where a small four-drawer dresser was tucked snug into the small closet. She opened the top drawer where Rene's clothing lay neatly folded.

Jim looked at the open drawer and said, "I know about this. I wondered if you had found it yet. I saw her hanging his clothes on the line years ago, and I asked her about it. I debated telling you then but decided not to."

"Well, that's not the whole story. I don't know, maybe you know about the rest, too?"

"What story? No, I just know about the clothes."

She opened up the next three drawers. They were filled to the top with songs Margaret had written on lined paper.

"Holy smokes! What the hell?" Jim cried. "These are hers? She wrote songs? I didn't know she wrote songs. Did you?"

"Well, yes, I knew she dabbled in it when she was younger from what Aunt Bea told me, and she used to play in pubs in Calgary and sing her own compositions. That I remember, before Papa got sick."

"Oh, yeah," Jim said. "I do recall her going to Calgary and performing in a pub, and of course, singing in the choir and at kitchen parties, but I don't remember her saying she actually wrote songs."

"I mean this is crazy. There must be over a hundred songs here. There is also a box on the upper shelf with a tape recorder, and I'm sure over fifty cassette tapes," she said as she pointed to the shelf above the dresser. "And, get this, there was a letter. I have it in the living room. It was sitting on top of Papa's clothing. It was addressed to you, me, Alex, and Sandy."

Jim looked off into space.

"What is it, Jim?"

"BB, this is what she was saying before she died. Oh, my God, I never said anything because it didn't seem to make sense."

"What do you mean?"

"Her last word was *dresser* BB. I... I never told you because... oh, I just assumed I had misunderstood her."

She touched his arm, "It's okay, not to worry, I would have found it eventually anyway. Look, it's already seven o'clock. Want to stay for supper? I was thinking of ordering take out—I have a craving for ginger beef from Wong's Chinese Restaurant. I've not had it in years, that and a couple of bottles of wine. Then we can read the letter together after we eat."

"Got it. Don't say another word. I'm on my way."

When Jim returned, they both walked to the living room and sat on the floor, their backs leaning on the couch in front of the fireplace. Lena Bea already had a fire going. They had often sat there as teenagers, snuggled up on a blanket, watching the fire and just talking for hours, kissing and discovering each other's bodies while Margaret slept soundly down the hall.

It had been drizzling all day, and the air was chilled. "I thought a fire would be nice to take the chill out of the room, and I found this blanket in my room that we used to sit on."

"Just like old times. I'll get some forks and wine glasses."

"I found these sympathy cards from Papa's funeral, and I wanted to read them first before burning them. A ritual, if you will."

They sat there taking turns reading the cards, eating and drinking wine. "Now here is one from a certain young man," Lena Bea piped up.

Dear Mrs. Gallant,

I'm so sorry about your husband's illness and his passing. I really loved Mr. Gallant. He was like a father to me in so many ways. He taught me how to fix things, tell a joke, make goat soap, ride a bike, and drive a tractor, among many other things. Being BB's best friend since grade one, I realize I probably spent more time at your house than at my own all these years. You and Mr. Gallant always made me feel welcome. I really miss him. And I want to again say how sorry I am. He was a great man.

Yours truly, Jim Heart

P.S. I'm here to help you anyway I can. So, don't worry, just ask me if you need anything.

"Oh, my God! That is so sweet! What sixteen-year-old boy would write something so beautiful? I don't remember ever reading this." She squeezed his hand and looked into his eyes. "I can't burn this one. It's too precious."

"Ahhh, it does sound sweet, doesn't it? I don't even remember writing that!"

The embers in the fireplace were dwindling. Jim put another log on the fire while she poured another glass of wine.

Lena grabbed the letter and sat down. "Okay, ready?"

"I'm all set."

Dear Lena Bea, Alex, Sandy, and yes, you too, Jim, my surrogate son,

I guess if you're reading this, I'm dead. After Jim caught me hanging Rene's clothing on the line, I decided I had better leave a letter to dispel any notions that I had lost my marbles. This is a revised edition I updated it in 1990 because I'm guessing I have been having some mini strokes. So, my time may be nearer than I anticipated.

By now you have found a drawer full of Rene's clothing, and I'm guessing around 150 songs (last count in 1990 anyways) I have written and some that I recorded on cassettes.

Let me explain why I kept it a secret and how these songs came to be.

Just before Rene got sick, I was at a point in my life where I thought I was finally going to get a chance at beginning to live my dream of becoming a professional singer- songwriter. I was finished with the pub scene and had just had a meeting planned with a well-known entertainer in Calgary, and also an invitation to perform at a music festival. Aunt Beatrice was here to help out at the farm and with Lena Bea. It was as if the stars were finally aligned. Ever since I was little girl, I felt I was destined to sing and write music and perform. It was a calling, if you will. Not something I chose. It was just who I was. Music somehow chose me. But in an instant, that dream fell apart. Rene became ill, and that was the end of it. Now don't get me wrong. I was happy to look after Rene till the day he died. I never saw it as a duty. It was one of the hardest things I've ever done, to watch someone I adored dwindle before my eyes. Looking back, I learned about true love, but it took a long while to realize it.

There were years of depression so deep that I didn't feel like I had a purpose anymore. Singing or playing music or writing songs was so far from my radar. In truth, I wanted to die most days.

Then, one day, I spoke to Mrs. Schmidt, and she gave me a little advice. She said, "Fake it till you make it." At first, I thought: how can I fake wanting to live when I feel dead inside? As long as I can remember there has been music playing in my head. I would hear music everywhere—in nature—the wind, in bird songs, even in the sounds of crickets and frogs—in the sounds from motors, or children's laughter. I could feel music inside my body and my mind. I could see it, and even smell it. There was never silence. There was never a time when music was not in me.

As Rene got sicker, I found it harder to sing. It felt forced. I quit the choir, the kitchen parties stopped, and the day he died there was a deadening silence. The music was gone completely. There was silence for the first time in my life, and death was all that I wished for. That went on for two years. Then I finally decided for the sake of those who loved me, especially my daughter, that I ought to give Mrs. Schmidt's advice a try.

I forced myself to write. I wrote anything that came to mind. I kept on writing, and writing, and writing. I wrote at night, and I never told a soul. Then one night, about three years after Rene had died, I went into the closet and found his clothing. I took his shirt and trousers out and placed them on the bed. I was thinking of packing them up and taking them to the Goodwill store. As I stared at his clothing a song came to me and it came fast. It was difficult to write it down as quickly as it was coming into my head. After I looked at it the next day, I thought to myself, "This is really good." Whether it was worth anything to anyone else or not was not a concern. It was called 'If I Could Fly.'

It is funny when I think about it. At one point in my life, I had a voice coach who told me I had to write from my soul. I had to dig deep inside me because that was where my true calling was, my inner genius, he called it. I understood what he meant but I never really was able to harness that inner genius until that night when I wrote 'If I Could Fly.'

Rene is my muse. I only have to look at his clothing and I see him, feel him, hear him laugh, and even smell him. And somehow, his presence triggers my brain and the songs come. Some fast, some take a little more time. The songs transformed me; they healed me from my depression; they helped me to see the purpose of life. Not just my life or Rene's life but life in general.

When I wrote these songs there was no goal in mind. What I mean is, I had no audience in mind. There was no ego involved. My dream of performing and being famous left the day I said goodbye to Rene. I have written all these songs because I'm a song writer. I wrote because I could not help it.

What you choose to do with them is totally up to you. They are my gift to all of you.

Love and hugs, Margaret Gallant, Mom, and Grandma

"BB, this is incredible! I had no idea, did you?"

"Not one iota."

"Now it makes sense. I used to see the lights on at her place late at night. She was always sitting at her desk. She was writing songs," Jim said.

"I don't know what we are going to do with this, Jim. It is addressed to you, me, and the kids. We need to think about it and figure out what, if anything, we do with it. Can we keep it just between us for now till we have some time to think about it and decide?"

"Absolutely, I agree. I propose a toast to Margaret and Rene," Jim said as he raised his glass of wine."

"To Mom and Papa!"

The next day . . .

"BB, I'll be over in a few minutes. I'm just running into town to get some cleaning supplies."

"Okay, see you in a bit."

Lena Bea heard a knock on the door. It was Sally and Paul, the young couple from down the road.

"Just on time!" Did you get a cattle trailer to load the goats?"

"Yes, we are good to go."

The goats and chickens, along with the soap-making equipment that hadn't been used in years, were all sold to Sally and Paul, who had just moved to the area a month before. When they heard that Margaret had passed away, they were one of the first to stop by. They told her that they had been living in Calgary for years, and when their third child was born, they had decided they wanted their kids to grow up in the country like they did. They met Margaret when she arrived on their doorstep the day they moved in. She introduced herself as part of the Welcome Wagon group. She brought freshly-baked sourdough bread, a jar of pickles, and some peas and beans from her garden along with a list of the names of neighbours with their telephone numbers and information on the town.

They visited back and forth, and Sally even got a lesson on making sourdough bread.

"I made my first loaf of bread the night before she died. You had an amazing mother, Lena Bea. She was one of a kind. We feel so lucky to have had her in our lives even for such a short time. Because of her, we felt so welcome in the community."

"Thank you, your words mean a lot to me. More than you know."

And it was true. Although she talked to her mother on the phone on a regular basis and visited when she brought Alex for his summer holidays at Grandma's and his once-a-month weekend sleepovers, they had never really talked about her day-to-day life, she realized. Starting with the letter, all the gifts, and cards, and letters from her aunt and others, and all the stuff she had gone through, she was beginning to see that she knew very little about her mother.

Jim and Lena Bea cleaned the house from top to bottom. The only things left were the bed, the couch, and a bit of food in the fridge.

"It's seven-thirty and time to quit BB. Supper is served. Bring the white wine from the fridge," Jim called from the living room.

They sat on the floor against the couch like the night before. After Jim's famous pasta salad and some chocolate cupcakes they found in the freezer, they poured some more wine.

"We smell like Mr. Clean!" Lena Bea said laughing.

"Maybe you do, I don't," Jim chuckled.

"Let me see." Lena Bea said as she leaned in close to him.

Their legs touched and Lena's entire body tingled. She touched his face. He reached for her and leaned in to kiss her without thinking. Without hesitation, Lena Bea's body responded with a fierceness she had never felt before. At his touch, electricity coursed throughout her entire being. He unbuttoned her shirt and kissed her neck and shoulders, and she pulled off his t-shirt. Their lovemaking was slow but intense and seemed to go on for an eternity. He kissed her scars from her terrible accident and with every touch, her body responded in rhythm with his. She rolled on top of him, their naked bodies in tune with each other and in perfect time until they climaxed together. "Oh, God, BB, how I missed you."

They laid on the blanket till four in the morning, only getting up to put more wood on the fire. They talked about their lives. They told each other their inner-most thoughts and their secrets: her accidents, her near-death-experience, his unhappy marriage, their children, and Robert's affairs. They teased each other, they laughed, and they cried. The only thing they omitted was talking about the fateful meeting years ago at the Post Hotel Pub in Lake Louise.

"I better go, it's a small town. The sun will be rising soon." Jim said as he stroked her hair.

She didn't want him to leave. But she knew he was right. As they stood at the back door, Lena Bea held his face in her hands.

"I don't remember ever feeling so loved as I do in this moment."

"Don't say it BB. We both know we have to go back to our lives, to our families. I'll never stop loving you."

She kissed him gently on the lips, then looked into his eyes and said: "Good-bye, Jim."

Her mother had specific instructions for what she wanted for her funeral. She reminded Lena Bea about them every few years. "Do you remember where my will is and instructions for my funeral?"

"Ma, I know. You've told me a thousand times. In the jewelry box that Papa made that is in your desk drawer."

Her mother was so organized! Even down to the poetry reading at her funeral. She was adamant she didn't want a eulogy. "Maybe just a few people coming up to say a few words. Nothing more." she had said. She wanted a simple service held at the funeral parlour. She called up Ken Smith, the local funeral director and set up a meeting.

"Ken, I have my mom's instructions for her funeral here." She took the envelope from her purse and handed it to him. He read the letter with the instructions, and then set it down on his desk ever so gently.

"Mrs. Kress, I mean Lena Bea, I have to be honest, I've been in the funeral business for over forty years, and I've known your mother that long. There is no way we can have her celebration of life service in the funeral home. She was a very popular woman in our community, and I'm ninety-nine percent sure that even the school gym is not going to be big enough. Also, I was thinking of having a live video on a screen for the people standing outside so they can see the celebration live. I have all the equipment. I also suggest that after the service we take the video to the hospital and senior's homes where she volunteered for those who are not well enough to attend the service."

"Really, Ken? Oh, gosh, I didn't even think of that. But you must know, this is your business."

"Yes, and I know this town. We are a very tight knit group, and she was a pillar of our little community."

"Pillar of the community? Really? It's not a phrase I would ever use to describe her. I mean she had her friends over for kitchen parties and she volunteered a bit, but a pillar?"

"Oh, yes. She was very well respected here. Very active in the community. I urge you to consider my suggestions. Folks would be mighty upset if they couldn't pay their respects. A funeral or any celebration of life service, is for the living. It is a way for people to begin to heal from their grief, to pay tribute to someone they cared about. It is so important. And may I add, without sounding presumptuous, you're a celebrity, Mrs. Kress, and there may be dignitaries coming from all over to support you, and I expect some press as well."

"I never thought about any of this. I trust your judgement, Ken. You know best. Just let me know what I need to do."

Ken was spot on. The school gym was full, there were people standing in the hall, and a big group watching a screen outside. The press was there and so were many of her friends and colleagues including Nancy Green and her husband, as well as Lena Bea's old coaches, many of whom she hadn't seen in years.

The one thing Lena Bea had insisted on was a simple service, like her mom had instructed. When the microphone was offered to anyone who wanted to say a few words, Lena Bea almost fell off her chair. People lined up around the perimeter of the gym. Her uncle Philip was the MC, and you could see the shock on his face when the line kept getting longer and longer. There were young people and old, even a few people in wheelchairs.

Lena Bea knew about her mother's kitchen parties, that she still sold her vegetables at the market, that she visited newcomers with Welcome Wagon and visited seniors, and that she sang in the community choir, but there was so much more Lena discovered that day. It seemed there was not a person in town whose life she had not touched in some way. There were so many stories about how she encouraged people to pursue their dreams and not give up. It was a theme that resonated throughout the entire service.

There were stories from students about the science trips she and Rene took them on and how those trips changed how they viewed the world. A very successful lawyer in Calgary told a story about how at school he was so shy he shook like a leaf if he had to say anything out loud in class. He told them how her mom, in one year as his teacher, encouraged him and helped him come out of his shell and gain confidence to the point that he decided to run for school council. What she taught him changed his life, and he owed it to her that he became successful.

A woman came up and took the microphone. Tears filled her eyes.

"Hello, my name is Frances Wagner. I flew from Ontario to be here today to send off one of the most important people in my life, next to my parents. When Margaret was in teacher's college, she had an assignment to come to Black Diamond in her second year. She stayed with our family. I was in grade two. I was the most inquisitive child Margaret had ever met, she told me that years later, although she also told me that I had some competition with her grandson, Alex. When we moved back to Ontario our family exchanged letters. Once my parents passed away ten years ago, I would have long talks with Margaret on the phone. I went to visit her when I was on an expedition in Alberta when I was forty years old. It was a visit I shall never forget. She told me stories about all the questions I asked and how I would walk to school with her every day and hold her hand. She encouraged me like no one else. I was so obsessed with nature and wanted to know everything. At twenty-three I became a paleontologist, and later I became a pioneer in the use of Micropaleontology to map Canada's terrestrial and marine geology. And I was a woman! I owed my success to Margaret. She encouraged me to follow my dreams and not to let anything or anyone stand in my way. To be honest, most people were just annoyed with my inquisitive nature, but Margaret told me it was a gift, and she taught me it was important to use that gift. I shall miss our late-night conversations and the letters that I so looked forward to. My last letter was just three weeks ago." She looked at the urn and bowed her head. "Fly high, my dear friend."

Lena Bea looked at Frances, dumbfounded. She might have heard her mother mention Frances a time or two in her life, but she had no idea they had such a close relationship.

Next, Mr. and Mrs. Wong, who were in their seventies and still working in their restaurant, came to the front holding hands. They began by singing a Chinese folk song, and then Mr. Wong said, "We taught that song to Margaret when she invited us to her and Rene's kitchen parties so very long ago. We taught it to her, and she tried so hard to sing it, but she had a very bad accent!"

To which everyone in the crowd laughed. Mrs. Wong continued, "Her heart was broken when Rene died, and ours was, too. When she started the kitchen parties again three years later, we were all very happy. Those parties were so much fun! We will miss her. She and Rene made us feel so welcome, and we never missed a kitchen party at their house. It has been the highlight of our lives." Then together they looked at the urn and said, "Zàijiàn."

Lena Bea was in awe. She looked around the room and saw people sobbing openly. There was hardly a dry eye in the whole gym.

Near the end, the whole community choir who had been standing in line, went up to the front and sang Vera Lynn's "We'll Meet Again." Lena Bea recognized it as one of the songs they often sang at their kitchen parties, just before everyone went home.

The service went on for over three hours, and Lena Bea was exhausted from crying and laughing. It was a wonderful service, and she knew her mother was looking on. Her whole view of who her mother was, changed that day. She stood waiting for Robert to get the car and watched as people left the gym. Her mind wandered to a conversation she had a year ago with her Aunt Beatrice. She came to stay with her in Calgary for a few days to get some dental work done. She had somehow forgotten the conversation, but it all came flooding back to her.

She described to her how her mother's childhood had been so difficult. How she was abused and had to hide her guitar from her father and practice playing on a piece of wood. That she wrote songs as young as eight years old, dreamt of being a famous singer-songwriter, and how every turn she took in life, squashed her dreams: her father's wrath, the convent, having to make a living by the age of sixteen, putting herself through teacher's college, and even how marriage and having a child had put her dream on hold. Then when the day arrived that she actually got her big break and things were looking like it was finally going to happen, her world fell apart. She could still remember her aunt's words.

"The day she found out your father had Lewy Body Dementia was also the first time she got a letter of acceptance to perform at the Calgary Kiwanis Music Festival. The only reason I know that is because I found the acceptance letter in the garbage when I was cleaning up. I never said a thing to her, and she never ever mentioned it to me."

Thinking about the conversation now, she remembered asking her aunt why she never told her about her life as a child and a young woman, why she hid it all from her own daughter. And her aunt said, "I don't know. She has always been secretive, a very private person. When your father got sick, she said to me, and I remember it vividly, 'I'm broken, Auntie, and I don't know if I can ever be put back together.' It was the saddest thing I ever heard in my life."

"And then she looked after papa for five years." Lena Bea added.

Lena Bea sipped her wine and sighed. "I remember the depression she fell into for years after he died. I was so angry at her for not being there for me. I swear she sat in her rocker looking out the window for two years. If it hadn't been for you and Jim, I don't know how I would have survived his illness and her depression. I was just so angry, and then I turned into an angry teenager, which was even worse! I was mad at her for years—I think until my skiing accident really."

"Yes, I knew you were angry and resentful. I felt sorry for you because it was like you had lost both parents there for a few years."

"Thank you for telling me all this. It helps. You of all people know we have had struggles in our relationship. I feel bad now that I wasn't more understanding all these years. She did the best she could under the circumstances."

As Lena Bea got into the car, an idea suddenly hit her. She knew what to do with her mother's songs. She would run it by Jim and see what he thought.

July 31, 1992

Lena got home from her meeting at the foundation in time to pack up a few things and get the kids in the car. She was going to pick Robert up at the airport, and then they were heading straight to their chalet in Canmore for a week. She thought it would do them all good to get out of the city and get some fresh air. She actually preferred the chalet to the penthouse but with the kids in so many activities, her foundation responsibilities, and the jazz quartet she played in, well, it was just more realistic to live in Calgary.

She saw Robert coming out of the airport. She realized he was more handsome now than he was before. He was forty-seven, but he only had a few grey hairs sprinkling his temples. His blonde hair and tanned skin seemed to bring out his baby-blue eyes even more. Not an ounce of fat on him. It was something he prided himself in.

"Perhaps too much," she thought. "He is so self-centred and shallow."

As he reached over in the driver's seat and kissed her, she smelled his familiar scent. The comfort it brought her always surprised her. "Comfort, yes, but not longing or desire like with Jim. Just comfort," she thought to herself.

"Kids asleep?"

"Yeah, they were out before I got here. Well, it's ten-thirty. We have a good drive yet. How did your marketing presentation go?"

"Great! I'm looking forward to being able to be home for a while, though. No more hotel rooms for at least a few more months, I think. I can snuggle up with you every night," he said as he winked at her.

"Does that mean his latest affair is over?" she wondered.

"How did it go with the movers?"

"They came right on time. Took the piano to the dementia ward at the hospital, and they were thrilled to pieces. The rest of the stuff went to the We Care Thrift Store. I took a few things to a storage place."

"I thought you said you didn't want to keep any stuff. You hate stuff," he said jokingly.

"I know, I know, but I couldn't part with the instruments, especially the beloved harmonica, and there were also a few little furniture pieces that I thought maybe we could use one day."

"What are you going to do with a bunch of instruments?

"I don't know, maybe Alex or Sandy will want them one day. You never know. Alex loves music. Maybe he'll take up the guitar."

They arrived at the chalet just on the edge of town. They had designed their place themselves. It was a 4000 square-foot, two-storey house made with giant western red cedar and nestled in a half-acre lot. The living room was an open A-frame that rose two storeys. The entire wall was windows except for the huge rock fireplace in the centre. The view was magnificent, not a neighbour in sight, only the view of the mountains as a backdrop to the beautiful spruce and fir trees and the trembling aspen that turned golden in the fall. Nestled into the rocks was the kidney-shaped pool and a hot tub. The house was bigger than what they first wanted, but they decided that with all the entertaining they did, they had better keep it to a similar size as their penthouse. So, they built a six-bedroom chalet, each bedroom with its own bathroom. Lena Bea did not like clutter, and she was very particular at decorating. She bought only high-end furniture with a nature theme, and mostly handmade by Canadian artists and designers. There were giant, modern art pieces hung on the walls that she never tired of admiring. Set in the southeast corner of the living room was a glorious, life-sized angel. It was only in their own bedrooms that she allowed any personal items like photos of the family, a cedar chest her father had made her, and on her dresser, the jewelry box her father had made for her mother that she had recently placed there.

Robert had insisted on an attached three-car garage and a shop where he could putter around. He loved his shop. His latest project, near completion, was a cedar canoe that he and Alex were building together.

The next evening after the kids were in bed, Lena Bea and Robert sat in the living room. She was on her fourth glass of wine. While he read a book in the corner chair, she sat on the sofa staring at the fire and reminiscing about the last few weeks. She looked over at him and suddenly felt like she wanted to throw up. She went to the bathroom and looked at herself in the mirror. She was sweating and felt shaky. "God, what have I done with my life?" she said to herself. "I can't stand my husband." She knelt on the floor and put her head over the toilet bowl and threw up. The vomit smelled like red wine. She sat on the floor, legs sprawled out, afraid to leave. She had drunk too much. Her head was pounding. She began to heave and grabbed the top of the toilet bowl and threw up again and again till there was nothing left. She cried, and then finally got up, brushed her teeth and gargled, and walked into the living room.

"I'm going to bed, I don't feel well," she told Robert.

"Okay, good night."

There was no, *can I get you anything, are you okay,* nothing, just *good night.* She had been in the bathroom for at least a half an hour and all he could say was *good night.*

Her legs felt weak and her head was still pounding a bit as she made her way to the bedroom. She fell onto the bed with her clothes still on, smelling the sour wine on her blouse. She stared up at the skylight. It was a clear night. There were so many stars and a beautiful crescent moon right in the centre of the skylight.

"I should be happy. I have everything I could possibly want. We are wealthy. I had an amazing career as an athlete. I have a foundation that I'm proud of that helps people. I have two amazing children. I have two gorgeous homes. I have no right to complain about my life," she thought to herself.

But after one weekend with Jim, it was as clear as the night sky that her love life had been an utter disaster from the beginning. There was only one man she had ever loved and that was Jim. She chose Robert not for love but for a way to advance her career. She was a selfish, egotistical monster.

She curled up in a ball.

She saw herself at seventeen years old, meeting Robert for the first time. She had been helping a little skier to his feet on the bunny hill at Lake Louise. She heard a loud scream and turned to see a teenage boy hit a tree. Robert was on the rescue squad and when he came to get the poor young boy, she told him what happened. The next day, they met on the ski hill and skied together.

She could tell Robert was infatuated with her the minute he saw her ski and before the month was out, he was taken with her. For her though, it was more gradual. If she was honest with herself, which she was trying to be more and more since she spent the weekend with Jim, she *did* like parts of Robert. He was charming in a way that people gravitated to him. But he was so caught up in his looks and his image that even then, at seventeen, there was a part of her that felt embarrassed to be seen with him in public. He was always boasting about how great he was, and even now she realized, he bragged about how he was responsible for her success. But to be fair, he *was* responsible for her success. Yes, she had the talent, but he was one who had the connections and made it all happen.

He would say over and over how he was *head over heels in love* with her, but even from the start, she caught him flirting with other women, many times right in front of her. Knowing him as she did now, he probably didn't even realize he was doing it. He just had this idea as long as she had known him, that he was God's gift to women.

They married quickly after meeting. She was just eighteen and he was nineteen. They had so many fights during the first few years of their marriage she wondered now how they ever stayed together. But she knew deep inside that it was because more than anything she wanted to ski in the Olympics, and he was her ticket. He talked her into becoming her manager, and in a way, it became a marriage of convenience, a payoff for both of them really. She got to the Olympics, and he got to be the big wig who made it all happen.

And he was good at managing her career. He could schmooze with the best of them, and he got more publicity for her than any other skier. He came up with the idea of starting a sports clothing line with her name on it, and he had basically run the business, and still did.

His father had inherited land that turned out to be rich in oil. They were wealthy and had connections with not only the socially elite, but also with the sporting elite because of their generous donations over the years. Nancy Green's coach was a good friend of his dad's. All it took was a simple phone call to get him to agree to watch her ski. So when she discovered that her new husband was actually having affairs, and not just flirting, she was in too deep. She needed him.

There was not a time, though, when she didn't wonder if she ever would have gotten into the Olympics if it hadn't been for him. She finally decided at one point that she would never know. She had the talent, but she didn't have the support, not even from her mother. She remembered being told by her coaches at school that she could most likely make it to the Olympic level as a skier with some work, the right coaches, and a lot of commitment and dedication, but her mom would have to be on board with it to make it happen. She didn't even bother asking her. Her mother always came home from teaching and sat in her rocking chair and stared into space, not saying a word more often than not. She didn't want to think about that again. In her gut she still felt resentment towards her mom, even after all that she learned about her life and all that she went through. She wondered if she would ever truly let those feelings go. It was always in the back of her mind. If her mom had been on board, she could have made it to the Olympics, and she and Jim would have married and grown old together. There would have been no need for Robert.

She finally got up and took a shower and a couple of aspirin. She decided it was better to sleep in another bedroom. She just couldn't sleep with Robert, not tonight. The more she thought about their life together and her weekend with Jim, the thought of Robert touching her felt wrong. She went to one of the guest rooms, closed the door, and locked it. She slid under the sheets and prayed for sleep, but it wouldn't come. Her mind drifted to her last competitive ski. It was February 13, 1976, at the Olympics in Innsbruck, Austria. She was in the best shape of her life and so sure she would place again in at least two more events. She had already won gold the day before. But the night before the second race, she decided to change her schedule a bit and she arrived in her hotel room an hour earlier than planned so she could get to bed early. She didn't call Robert because he said he was going to be in a meeting with the press till eight-thirty. She opened the door to their suite and saw the TV was on. It looked like a porn movie was playing. There was a woman with giant breasts and two guys having sex with her. Then she heard the sound of a woman's voice coming from the bedroom, clearly having sex. "Is the TV in the bedroom on a porn channel, too?" she wondered. Then it hit her, she must have walked into someone's else's room by mistake. She started to leave, embarrassed that she had walked in the wrong room, when out of the corner of her eye, she saw her jacket on the couch just where she had left it. Her heart began to race, and she could feel the adrenaline in her body as she swung open the bedroom door only to see Sheila, a reporter she had known for years, on all fours with Robert behind her. Sheila was screaming away: "Slap me again, Bobby, harder! Harder!" Robert's eyes were closed and he was grunting and slapping Sheila, totally oblivious to Lena Bea standing in the doorway.

"Are you two kidding! What the hell is going on here!" she screamed at the top of her lungs. Her whole body shook. Her heart was pounding so loud it felt like it would come out of her chest. "GET OUT BOTH OF YOU! NOW! GET OUT!"

They stopped. The look on their faces was something she could never erase. She knew Robert had affairs but that was the first time she had ever actually caught him in the act.

The next day, with little sleep, she skied the Alpine Downhill—her favourite race. She knew she was on her way to her second gold medal win, when all of sudden, near the tail-end of the race, an image of Robert and Sheila flashed before her eyes and her ski immediately slipped ever so slightly to the right, causing her to lose control. She could hear the crowd chanting, "Gutsy Lena, Gutsy Lena," and the next thing that she remembered was seeing a clump of trees racing towards her.

Watching the reruns on TV, she had to agree, it was a miracle that she had walked away. She had fallen a million times skiing but that time was different. It was a heavenly intervention, maybe her papa, that somehow saved her from not breaking her neck. The only sustained injuries were two broken ribs and a permanent hearing loss from the concussion she suffered when her head collided with the trunk of a spruce tree.

The fall was enough to convince her to quit competitive skiing for good. She had achieved way beyond her goals in the ten years she had skied professionally. She didn't want to push her luck. She knew she had let her emotions from the night before the fall sabotage her impeccable concentration. Robert begged her not to quit and promised to never have another affair, but she knew it was the end of her career and most likely her marriage.

The news of her retirement hit the headlines. "Why are you retiring, Lena?" the reporter asked.

"In this sport, you can't hesitate, not when you ski at lightning speed. And after that fall, I guess my "gutsiness," as everyone calls it, is just gone. I don't want to tempt fate, and so I'm retiring. It has always been my dream to start a foundation to support children in sports who don't have the financial means to pursue *their* dreams. I'm looking forward to beginning that new chapter in my life."

Robert convinced her to forgive him and start over. And she had to admit even now thinking back, that their marriage was the best it had ever been after that night. He was attentive, and as far as she could tell, he was faithful. They developed the sports clothing line, and set up the foundation, and began building the chalet in Canmore. She felt her life was back on track. They were happy and busy for two years. Then she was in another accident that changed everything. She played it over in her head as she had done a million times.

She and Robert, and his brother Danny, who was married to her best friend Jenny, decided to go spring skiing at Lake Louise. They were taking their time, leisurely going down the hill. She was trying to show Jenny how to lean into her turns a little better and they started to laugh.

"Lena, there is no way I can lean anymore. My ski suit is so damn tight that I can barely bend my knees. How did I get so fat since last winter?"

"Humm, I wonder…" Lena Bea said, smiling over at Jenny.

Even though they met at Lake Louise, Jenny rarely skied. She worked at the chalet and they met in the dorm where they lived. She was the first real girlfriend she had ever had, and they became best friends instantly. When Jenny stood up for her at her wedding, she met Robert's brother Danny, and within a year they, too, were married.

Danny was nothing like his older brother. He was a quiet, shy man and Robert was his idol. Jenny and Danny already had a two-year-old son and Jenny had just confided in her that she suspected she might be pregnant again, but she hadn't gone to get tested yet.

"Mum's the word, Lena, I haven't even told Danny yet."

"No worry, your secret is safe with me. But it would be nice for Alex to have a sister or brother. I know growing up as an only child I wanted a sibling so bad. But then I found you!"

"I know, you're the sister I never had, too. Being an only child, what were our parents thinking?" she laughed.

They were both laughing hard when, without warning, they heard what sounded like thunder behind them. Lena Bea turned and saw a cloud of snow coming down the mountain. She screamed, "Oh, God! Go right! Go right!" But it was too late. Within a second an avalanche hit them, and she and Jenny began tumbling, their skies flying in the air. She still remembered glimpsing Jenny's purple skis and hearing a pounding in her ears that resonated throughout her body. And then in a few seconds, dead silence.

Robert told her later how he had watched in horror as she, Jenny, and Danny were swept away and how all he could see was the occasional ski through the blinding snow. He was the only one in their group that was not in the line of the avalanche.

Later he would tell her, "When it happened, I thought you all had to be dead. But there you were with your head above snow, and you were breathing. I left you there and searched for Jenny and Danny. It seemed impossible. The snow was so deep. Others joined me and we were all running on adrenalin, frantically screaming their names and digging with our bare hands. When we found Jenny, I knew right away that it was not good. Her neck was clearly broken, and she was dead. The rescue squad came quickly, and we all searched and searched for Danny but where I thought he was we found nothing. We searched till dark. The next morning the rescue squad found Danny's body buried deep in the snow nowhere near where I thought he was."

Lena Bea didn't remember being taken to the hospital or anything about that time until she woke up after her near-death experience. And when she came to, the pain was so intense she wished that she was back in the other realm where there was no pain. She had internal bleeding, had lost her spleen, broken her pelvis and several ribs, and had shattered her left elbow. The morphine, although it helped with the pain, was of little help dealing with her emotions after finding out that her best friend and brother-in-law didn't survive. A week later as she lay in her hospital bed, Robert came into the room, his face white as a ghost.

"What is it, Robert? What is wrong?"

"I just came from the reading of Jenny and Danny's will. They said should they both die; they wanted you and I to raise their children." He paused. "Lena, we have custody of Alex if we so choose. If not, he becomes a ward of the court."

"Oh, my God! Yes, yes. Of course." Lena said, through the tears running down her face.

"That is what I thought, too. I told the lawyer I had to ask you, but I was sure it was a yes. He will bring the papers to the hospital tomorrow. We are going to be parents," he said as he kissed her hand.

An image of her and Jenny at the Glenbow Gallery when Jenny had her art show, came into her mind. Walking arm in arm around the gallery before the doors opened, they giggled like they were school girls. She was as excited as Jenny was. It had taken a long time to get the recognition she deserved but when it came—which was only weeks before the gallery show—it was instant. Within a few weeks she was getting calls from London and New York galleries wanting her pieces. The press was calling and she was doing interviews on morning talk shows and in art magazines. She was unique, and she was charismatic. The public loved her.

Lena Bea cried. She vowed to keep her memory alive for Alex.

Until she was discharged from the hospital Jenny's parents kept Alex most of the time, and Robert spent as much time with him as he could. Finally, four months later, when she walked out the hospital doors, she finally got to hold Alex and take him home for good.

Being a mother was easier than she had thought it would be. It felt natural. And with two sets of grandparents and her own mother all helping out when Robert was away on business or when she was at her rehab appointments, it was easy. But what became evident early on was that Alex was happiest when he was with her mother. When Alex woke up in the mornings, he was asking for Grandma Margaret more often than not. Gramma Margie, he called her. "Where is Gramma Margie? I love Gramma Margie. I want to see her. I miss her," he would say.

In a way, she was happy. She loved her in-laws, but they were not much into being grandparents. They were wealthy and they traveled a lot to Palm Springs and Europe, and when they were home, they were always socializing with friends or playing tennis or skiing.

Jenny's folks were nice people, but after Jenny died, they were so distraught, and they both began to drink excessively. When she took Alex over to their house, it seemed the only thing they did was sit in the living room and watch TV and feed him junk food. Although, to be fair, they did read a lot of books to him. But when she would pick him up, she could smell the beer and cigarettes on Alex's clothes, and it bothered her. Alex seemed happy enough with them and was always sad to leave, and they clearly loved him and had a bond, but she didn't feel good about leaving him in that environment very often and if Robert had his way, Alex would not have gone over to their house at all.

But she got it. They probably would never get over losing Jenny. There had been something special about her. She had been such a loving person and so bubbly all the time, and there was no one who could light up a room like she could. She was fun, and vibrant, and easy going. When she and Danny got together it was funny to witness how he would suddenly transform from a man who was as quiet and shy as a church mouse, to a man who had confidence and charisma. She was like a generator for him, giving him this boost of energy and confidence. In fact, she was like that for a lot of people, especially her parents. She suspected that little Alex had the same effect on people that his mother had. She definitely saw it with her own mother. The minute Margaret met Alex she transformed into the mother she remembered as a kid. She started to laugh again. She hadn't heard her mother laugh since her papa got sick.

She missed Jenny and often found herself talking to her in her mind, knowing that somehow, she was listening. The funny thing was, she got signs from her—feathers in places where there should not be feathers: like her laundry room, her office, parking lots, and downtown streets, and always when she felt alone and needed a friend it seemed. The feathers made sense. Jenny had been obsessed with feathers. She had used feathers in every one of her art pieces. She mainly painted but her sculptures were her best work, and when she died Lena Bea bought as many as she could find. She used feathers that people sent her from all over the world.

Her favourite piece was the life-sized angel with wings made with real feathers that she had electroformed with copper. The halo was made with citron crystals. Unfortunately, it had already been sold but she begged the couple who bought it to sell it to her so she could someday give it to her son. Thankfully, they agreed, but it cost her twice as much as they had paid for it. She didn't mind. It would go to Alex one day, and she couldn't imagine anyone else having it except him.

The days and months after the accident were a blur. One thing she remembered very clearly was that her mom was there by her side the whole time. The first year she took off teaching to drive her to appointments and take Alex to the farm almost every weekend. And if she would have had her way, she would have had him with her for the entire summer on the farm.

She rolled over in bed and sobbed. "Mom, you were my saving grace! God, I miss you," she whispered, softly looking out the window of the bedroom and trying to picture her mother's face.

She finally fell asleep and dreamt of feathers falling from heaven.

The next morning, Lena Bea was in the kitchen making breakfast for the children. Sandy was colouring in her colouring book at the table, and Alex was telling her about the project he was working on for the science fair. Robert walked in and gave her a dirty look and said, "Sleep well, Lena?"

"Yes, actually I did. It took a while to fall asleep, though. I was feeling pretty sick if you really want to know."

"What seems to be the problem now?"

"Excuse me?"

"Please don't fight," Alex pleaded.

"We are not fighting, Alex. Now sit down and eat."

Robert left the room, and she heard the door slam. She was not surprised. He never understood when she was in pain, emotionally or physically. She sat down at the breakfast nook and pretended to read a magazine. Inside, she felt the anger rising like steam. Robert never empathized with what she was going through. Not even after the avalanche accident. She had not only lost her best friend and become a mother overnight, but her doctors told them she was going to live in chronic pain for the rest of her life. And his response was, "You're a trooper, kiddo, you'll come out of this with flying colours. You have more guts than Carter's got liver pills."

"But you don't get it," she told him over and over.

"I don't get it? I lost my little brother. What exactly don't I get? I'm hurting, too. But life goes on, and we have a son to raise."

"I know, I know. You lost your brother. I am so sorry. I understand that you are hurting. It's just that I'm living in so much damn pain all the time on top of our loss and becoming parents. The constant pain wears me down and I have no one to talk to about it. I need to talk about it! I need to be able to express how I feel to you."

"I don't know what you want me to say or do, Lena, that will help. I have a hard time listening to you complain all the time. I'm sorry, but your complaining is what wears me down!" he shouted.

It was while she was recovering from the accident that Robert had another affair. He was careless about it, coming home reeking of perfume, so it didn't take much to figure it out.

"I'm sorry, Lena, I'll break it off. I really don't know how it happened. It was just sex, nothing more, you know you're the only one for me."

She was devastated and so embarrassed and angry with herself more than anything, for believing that he would ever change.

But the affair didn't last long. Apparently what Robert's friend finally admitted to her with much prompting, was that when the woman realized he was married and his wife was recovering from a major accident, it was she who dropped him like a hot potato.

He charmed his way into gaining her forgiveness, and then things were better than ever once again.

She knew it was a pattern, and that it would just be a matter of time until he did it again, but she felt helpless and exhausted, and she just didn't have the energy to fight. And the thing was, he did excel at being a father. He still boasted, but now he boasted to everyone about his son and how smart he was, and how he was going to teach him everything about nature, fishing, hunting, camping, mountain climbing, and canoeing. Alex was clearly in awe of him, too, and even though he was gone a lot of the time on business, when he was home, it was Daddy, Daddy, Daddy. It was strange, but somehow it made her happy to see them together. Then without planning, sweet little Sandy came along.

It was not an easy birth. At forty-one she was old to be pregnant for the first time but the new IUD which her doctor said was, "the latest and greatest form of birth control," had failed. She was so sick the whole pregnancy, and the emotional rollercoaster of having to remove the IUD and risking miscarriage took its toll. On top of it, Sandy was breech and the birth was rough, to say the least. Her body had been through so much that she had decided she didn't want to get pregnant. But when she had, she remembered the last conversation she and Jenny had about wanting a sibling. It was like a sign, and she knew she had to go ahead with the pregnancy.

Thankfully, after Sandy was born, her mom was there to help because she could see Robert was not present mentally again. She was in no shape to have sex for over a year, and she knew in her heart his eyes were wandering. In fact, her friends would even tell her that they had seen him with other women.

"Oh, that's just Robert, he's a charmer, and the woman fall all over him. He's fine," she would say, knowing all along that he was having affairs. But when she confronted him, he always denied it. When she looked back, she was too exhausted to deal with it, and so she ignored it. It became easier to make excuses rather than confront him anymore. She felt stuck. If he hadn't been such a good father to Alex, she told herself over and over, she would have left him. But she just couldn't do it to Jenny's son, her son. Alex was a well-rounded, kind, sweet child. He would be devastated if he lost another parent. She couldn't do that to him.

She got up from the table and washed the dishes, shooing Alex and Sandy outside to play in the pool. She thought of her mom, happily reunited with the love of her life, her beloved Rene, out there somewhere in the other realm. Meanwhile she was here living a lie, sleeping beside a husband she now realized like a ton of bricks falling on her, that she didn't love and knowing that she would be reliving her weekend with Jim for eternity. Her memories of a solitary weekend now the closest thing she would ever have to true love.

1995

The week before, the chinook winds had melted all the snow and left slush in the streets. Cars were filthy with grime, and the drains in the street couldn't keep up with the melting. Then, as fast as the chinook came, it left, and the roads turned into solid ice. But it was Valentine's Day, and the restaurants were filling up, just the same as every other year. Michael, the *maitre'd* at La Petite Maison greeted Lena Bea and Jim as they entered. Bowing slightly forward, he said, "Welcome, Miss Lena Bea and Jim, and may I congratulate you on your first anniversary. It's hard to believe it has been one year since you brought your families here for your wedding reception. My, how time flies."

"Yes, it has gone quickly. Thank you, Michael. It's nice to be back." Jim said as he helped Lena Bea remove her coat and scarf.

"May I say, Madame, you look stunning this evening, and there is a beautiful glow to the two of you, even though it is freezing cold outside."

"Why, thank you," said Lena Bea. She did feel wonderful; it was not only their first wedding anniversary; they were also celebrating the final signing of the papers for The Gallant Kitchen Foundation.

"This way, please, I have the perfect table for you this evening." Michael said.

As they neared the table, they saw two red roses and tiny hearts sprinkled all over the table. A bottle of champagne was in an ice bucket.

"For our special guests, please enjoy your evening," Michael said, and with a bow he drifted off.

"Did you order this?" asked Jim.

"No, I thought you did. How sweet. That's why I love coming here. The service is impeccable."

Jim poured the champagne before they even looked at the menu. He lifted his glass and looked into Lena Bea's eyes. "A toast to my brilliant, beautiful, charming wife, and to me, the happiest man on earth." They clinked their glasses.

"Yes, to us!" she said with a smile.

"And another toast to The Gallant Kitchen Foundation, and to Margaret and Rene," she said.

They looked upwards and clinked again. Lena Bea knew if her mother and father were looking down on them, they would be smiling at the sight of the two of them there together.

As they talked about the foundation, Lena Bea wondered if Jim, whose life ambition was only to have a family and live a simple life in a small town, would be truly happy in her world. She had hoped she made it clear from the start that she didn't expect him to be like Robert when they were out in public. Robert, with all his faults—and there many—was a great conversationalist, and the one at a party that everyone wanted to speak to because he was a people connector. If you wanted to meet a person, he was sure to know them and happy to introduce you. Jim was shy, reserved, patient, and polite but not outgoing. In a way, Robert made it very easy for her to get things done and meet the people she needed to make connections with. Since he was no longer in the picture, she wondered if she and Jim could really pull off the new foundation and make it as successful as the one she and Robert had run. There was a lot of work ahead of them, and without Robert, it would be a different story this time around for her. But she didn't want Jim to concern himself with all the logistical nightmares that lay ahead in order to pull it off. She knew in time he would find his place in the company. It was a good thing she was older and wiser this time around, she had learned a lot about how to be patient and trust in the universe.

"I'm so excited about this foundation. It was a lot of work getting the copyright for 172 songs and setting it up, but I can't wait to get started. I think Ethan will be terrific at pitching the songs to artists and record labels. He told me yesterday that he had some big-name artists in the U.S.A. that would be the perfect fit for some of mom's songs. He came highly recommended. I get goose bumps thinking that we will hear mom's songs on the radio one day."

"What about the scholarship program? When does that get under way?" asked Jim.

"Well, I think that will be up and running within the year. If we just copy the way it was done with my Support for Sports Foundation it shouldn't take too long."

"It was a brilliant idea, BB. I just wish I could be more hands-on, but it is a big learning curve for me," said Jim with a frown.

She grabbed his hand. "Please, if there's one thing I've learned with my foundation over the years, it is to hire professionals who know what they are doing, and then learn from them. It was something that Robert always insisted on, and he was right."

"I have some other news," he said as he folded and unfolded his napkin, looking nervously at Lena Bea.

She squeezed his hand gently. She could feel his leg trembling under the table. "Jim, what is it?"

"My son, Nicholas, and his girlfriend, Barb, are getting married. He called me today. And, they are going to have a baby, so the wedding is in a month."

"That is wonderful! Congratulations!"

"Yes, it is wonderful, and I'm so happy for them. But, well… they are worried about Patricia and how we will get along at the wedding. I guess Pat is not pleased about us. Nicholas said he was afraid it would be too awkward having us both there."

"Awkward? She is the one who went to Yellowknife, had an affair, and never came back. I'm sorry, am I missing something here?"

"Well, from what Nicholas told me, she told him I had the affair first. I... I never said a word to anyone about us, and I know you didn't, so I don't know how she found out. And then Nicholas said I obviously lied. That she left me because I was having an affair with you. And the fact that we got married so fast after Robert died is proof. She told him we were having an affair ever since I moved to Millarville."

"Oh, for heaven's sake. What did you say to that?"

"I told him the truth. That we had a weekend together after your mom died and that was the end of it till a month before we got married. Gosh, BB, talking to my son about our weekend affair and all this. It was strange and awkward to say the least."

"I'm sure it was. Well, I guess Pat figured it out—well, a small part of it. Perhaps someone did see us and told her. Who knows? Not much we can do about that now. But saying you had the affair first is just her being spiteful. And I'm so sorry you had to go through that today of all days. But let's get back to the issue at hand. They're afraid it will be awkward to have us go to the wedding, and you're afraid she might act out at her son's wedding?"

"Yes. But they didn't come out and say *don't come*."

"What do you want to do?"

"I want to go, of course. He's my son, but I know Pat, and she can be quite vindictive. I would hope she would behave at her son's wedding, but truthfully, I'm not sure."

"Jim, you know what you need to do."

"I know. I need to call her and just talk to her instead of going through all the different scenarios."

"We cannot control how she behaves in the long run. We can only control how we act. Right?"

"I know you're right. I just needed you to remind me."

"Honey, I'll be by your side, and I'm a big girl. I'm the queen of putting on a face. I had to, living with Robert all those years. I can handle this. She will not get to me. And you, well, you're not one to lose your cool. I think we will be just fine. Nicholas knows the truth, and that is what really matters."

She grabbed his hands and looked into his eyes. She remembered how they had stood shivering in the cold on the porch swing of her house the first time they ever kissed, him with his braces and awkwardness, and his leg trembling to beat the band, and her so full of confidence, holding his face and feeling him melt when their lips touched.

"Gosh, I love you, BB."

"I know, and I couldn't be more in love with you even if I tried. We are going to be just fine. And, hey, we're going to be grandparents! How great is that?"

Lena Bea was watching Jim sleep. They had made love and he was sound asleep, his legs intertwined with hers. She was so content but a feeling of guilt came over her like a wave. Robert was dead. It was as if he had to die for her to be truly happy. She thought back to the fateful day.

It was snowing lightly, and as the large snowflakes hit the pavement, they melted. The roads were clear and the weather balmy for New Year's Eve. There was blue sky in the distance, and Lena Bea hoped that it meant the weather would stay nice. She was anticipating a stressful few days, and it would be nice not having to fight the elements. It was a bad stretch of road between Calgary and Lake Louise. The highway was infamous for having the most fatalities in all of Alberta. She just wanted the evening to be over with so she could get on with her new life with Jim. But she decided that she would do it after the Support for Sports Foundation's biggest event of the year—the New Year's Eve Charity Ball.

Normally it was an evening that Lena Bea looked forward to. She liked being in the limelight. She got to thank all the people who had donated to the foundation and made it possible to help children pursue their passions in sport. And not just children in Canada, but children in countries all over the world. But this year she was not looking forward to it at all. She was rehearsing in her head how tomorrow morning when they got home, she was going to tell Robert she was ending their marriage.

When she got to the podium, she was grateful for all the public speeches she gave over the years. She cleared her head of her thoughts about the next day, and then gave her speech without a hitch. Then it was just a matter of eating the meal and making small talk with the people at her table, and then a little dancing and chatting it up with a few people and it would be over.

She and Robert were sitting at the head table waiting for their second course to arrive when Adrian Boyle, the news anchor and newest member to her board of directors, came up to Robert and kissed him on the lips in front of everyone. Lena Bea had overheard someone at the office a month before say that he was having an affair with her. When she had confronted him that evening, he had sworn it was a one-night stand and it was over. But clearly it wasn't.

The room fell silent as all eyes stared at Robert and Lena Bea. Lena Bea had been humiliated before by Robert, but this time was different.

She rose from the table, and with as much grace as she could muster, said, "If you will all excuse me," and slowly walked out of the room, feeling 250 pairs of eyes following her. She went to the hallway and called Jim.

"Can you come and pick me up. I'm done here. I'll explain later."

Robert was killed instantly when a semi jack-knifed in front of him on New Year's Day at 11:02 a.m., just outside Banff National Park. He was forty-nine years old.

BOOK FOUR

Sarah, age four

"How did you learn all those songs, Sarah?"

"I made them up when I was that girl with the red hair."

"You wrote those songs? Who taught you to write songs?"

"Oh, I don't know. I just made them up in my head."

"Where did you live when you made up songs?"

"On a farm, some I made up when I was little, and some I made up when I was big."

SARAH
2014

Sarah listened to Alex as he talked nonstop in the car on the way to his parents' place. They had been dating for four months, and he explained to her that he had never brought a woman home for Christmas before.

"I want you to be prepared. My stepdad is very quiet, and some people think he is stand-offish. But he's a good guy. It was kind of weird that they got married so fast after Dad died but they had been childhood sweethearts, and I knew him growing up, and he was always really nice to me and my grandma. And Mom, well, you'll like her. Did I tell you that Mom was an Olympic skier?"

"Yes, you did, bunny. But you never told me much about her career."

"I'm sure she will be thrilled to tell you all about it. She had a pretty amazing career, but then she had two serious accidents. The first one was when she fell at the Olympics, which made her quit skiing competitively. The second was an avalanche, which I already told you about, when my birth parents died. She is an awesome mom. She has told me stories about my birth mom ever since I was little, so I feel like I know her."

"You have gone through a lot, Alex, and yet I haven't seen any evidence of scarring. No woe is me. Is it because of your mom?"

"Well, there is some scarring. It was hard when Dad, my adopted dad I mean, died soon after my grandma. I had a lot of anger. I let it build up and in my teenage years... Well, let's just say I'd like to forget them. I got into trouble with the law—stealing and drugs. I was one messed-up kid for a while. I hit rock bottom when one of my buddies committed suicide. It took that to make me realize that I needed to change. I got introduced to Buddhism by our neighbour in Canmore, and I started practicing and going on retreats. I even spent a year at an ashram in Nova Scotia. It saved me. I really found peace, inner peace. The scars are pretty well all healed. But to answer your question, was it because of Mom? In a way it was. She was so supportive of me, even when I was being a jerk. She never gave up on me. She would just say, 'You'll figure it all out. You're smart and the most loving person I know. You're just a little lost, and I get it.' I can still remember that as plain as day. And, of course, she was right."

"She sounds like a very smart woman and a great mother."

"She was and still is. You'll see."

Sarah wasn't nervous. If his mom was even remotely like he described, she knew she was going to love her.

"It was funny," she thought, "but the minute she met Alex it was as if she was home." She couldn't think of another way to describe it. She remembered the day vividly, probably because she had played it over and over in her head. It was the best day of her life.

It was her first rafting trip, even though she grew up near Canmore. It was a requirement for the "Banff Musicians in Residence Program," she was in. The visiting creative director wanted them to go out and experience nature in the raw, and one of the exercises was to go on a raft trip on the Nahanni River with Canmore Wilderness Adventure Tours. She really had to psych herself up because she didn't like going on or near the water since her parents' death. She was assured that this particular tour was not white-water rafting but a leisurely float on the river, but she was still hesitant.

"Welcome, my name is Alex Kress, and I'll be your guide today."

Sarah was picking out a life jacket, her back turned, when she heard his voice. It sounded familiar. "I must know him," she thought.

She turned around. She saw his face. It was like someone knocked the wind out of her.

Their eyes locked. It was the strangest, most wonderful feeling.

Four hours later, over a mocha at the cafe beside Alex's Wilderness Adventure Store, Alex blurted out: "So where have you been? I've been looking for you for years."

Sarah looked at him and wondered how, in only a matter of minutes, the script of her life could be totally rewritten. From being single and free and loving it, to wanting to spend the rest of her life with a man she had met only a few hours ago.

Sarah laughed.

"Okay. That might be the best pick up line I've ever heard, Mr. Smooth."

But in her heart, she knew she felt the same way. It was surreal; as they talked it was as if they knew each other's thoughts.

"I feel like someone matched us up at birth or something," she thought.

"I want to know everything there is to know about you, the unabridged version. I want to know it now. Tell me," Alex said.

"How about we go on a second date, er... I mean a first date first?" She laughed. "I'll make dinner at your place. My place right now is a dorm! You supply the wine, organic of course, and some nice ambiance?"

"Deal! And may I seal it with a kiss?" And, without waiting for a 'yes,' they both leaned over the small wooden table and kissed ever so gently.

"You even smell good," she said and smiled, her eyes glued to his. "Did I really just say that out loud?"

"Yup, you did," he said with a grin.

"Get a hold of yourself, girl," she told herself.

Freida, the owner of the cafe and a good friend of Alex's, saw the kiss. She did not advertise it, but she had inherited a gift of seeing people's auras. She could not help it. It was as natural to her as seeing shadows. She knew Alex's usual aura; it was mostly a beautiful green that meant he had a love of people, nature, and animals. But as she watched them kiss, a bright pink outlined by an iridescent white surrounded the two of them—something she rarely saw. It meant eternal love.

Many months later, Alex confided to Sarah what Freida had told him the next morning after seeing them kiss in the cafe.

"Not a word of a lie, Sarah, this is what she said to me. "Well, look at you my dear friend, you have fallen in love with your soul mate!" He explained that Freida was always a bit strange, but he thought she nailed it on the head.

She thought so, too.

That evening Sarah arrived at his "chalet," as he called it. It was just at the edge of town near the river. As she drove into the driveway, she saw the top of the huge, green sloped metal roof overlooking the river. There was an attached triple-car garage with the same type of roof and a row of black, glass windows across the doors. The main door was a large, double door with two life-sized angels carved into the wood. She wondered if she was at the right address. It didn't look anything like she pictured. She was expecting a small log house, not an artsy West Coast modern home

She rang the doorbell and heard him yell, "It's open!"

She walked in with two bags of groceries and set them down on the granite counter. She could hear Diana Krall's *Love Scenes* album playing in the background. The entire living room and dining room were windows that stretched up over forty feet and met with cedar beams that lined the ceiling. Through the giant, sliding glass doors, she saw twinkling white lights amongst the trees and blue lights around the hot tub. He was lighting candles on the table outside and among the rocks. She heard the sound of the river and saw the mountains in the distance. There was a freestanding stone fireplace in one corner of the living room and a life-sized angel sculpture in the other.

Her jaw dropped as she took in the spectacular view of her surroundings. She smelled lavender and noticed a cone-shaped mister near the entrance. She was not expecting anything even remotely as romantic as this. She breathed deeply, closing her eyes and soaking in the ambience.

The professional gourmet kitchen had huge sub-zero high-end stainless-steel appliances that included two wall ovens, a gas stove, and a double drawer dishwasher. There was a wine-rack the whole length of the wall and cookbooks on the shelves. It was an open concept with only cedar beams dividing the rooms. The oversized teal-coloured couch and pink buffet—with hand-painted cockatoos on it—popped out against the white shag carpet. He had giant plants growing everywhere, and she spied an Onni wood oven in the backyard surrounded by what looked like an outdoor kitchen. She didn't want him to notice how shocked she was at the extravagance of his place, and so she tried to keep the awe out of her voice and hoped she sounded casual.

"Nice place! I really love your angel sculpture."

"Thank you, my birth mother was an artist, and this is one of her pieces."

"She was extremely talented. I love the electroformed copper wings and the crystals. I have never seen anything quite like it."

"You can tell you're an artist by the way you look at how the piece was made. I don't think anyone has ever mentioned the electroforming technique."

He led her to the living room and pointed to the backyard. "I worked all day on the ambience. What do you think?" he asked.

"I'm overly impressed so far, but I'm trying to hide it." She laughed. "So, what do you cook in your Onni Oven? I was just looking at buying one. I love making pizzas with the thin crusts."

"Well, to be honest, I make sourdough bread in it. Our family is famous for our sourdough bread."

"You make sourdough bread? You're full of surprises, Alex."

They walked into the kitchen, and he poured them each a glass of wine. She began taking the groceries out of the bag and placing them on the counter. As he handed her a glass of wine, he leaned in and kissed her gently on the cheek.

"I'm so happy you didn't stand me up because I swear there has not been a moment that I haven't thought about you. I feel like I'm losing my grip on reality or something. Oh, God, I swore I wouldn't say a word, but seeing you seems to turn me into a blabber mouth."

"I have not thought about anything except you either, so no worries, Alex. The feeling is mutual." She held his face with her hands and looked into his baby-blue eyes, then slowly kissed him. He responded with a gentleness that nearly took her breath away.

"Okay, if we're going to eat, we'd better stop this right now," she said.

"I think you're right."

They both laughed.

Sarah taught him to make sushi rolls, and tempura, and miso soup. She used beets, asparagus, portabella mushrooms, sprouts, sweet potatoes, and mangos and strawberries. The meal was an art piece.

"I can't eat it," he said when they sat down at the table in the backyard.

"Why?"

"It's too pretty. I'm sorry. I feel like I should be taking a picture of it, not eating it. In fact, I think I'll take a picture with the two of us sitting here. I don't want to ever forget this moment."

He got up and went to the living room to get his camera, then set it up on a tripod and put on the timer. In the picture you could see Sarah with her strawberry-blonde hair up in a bun, loose strands and long bangs falling around her face, her dark blue eyes sparkling, tiny freckles covering her face and neck, and one small dimple on the left side of her face that only showed when she was smiling. She had on a black t-shirt with a purple and blue mandala on the front and a crystal-point necklace on a leather string. Alex had his arm around her shoulder, the sides of their faces touching ever so gently. His curly, long hair rested on her shoulder. His baby-blue eyes looked like they were grinning right along with his wide smile. He had on a black t-shirt, too, and it said, *Enjoy the Journey*. In the background were little white lights. In the foreground were candles, a beautiful multi-colored sushi platter, and two glasses of wine.

It was a photo they framed and hung in their bedroom after they got married.

They ate, and laughed, and talked. He told her about Shambala meditation and about his time spent at the Ashram in Nova Scotia where Pema Chodron, a Tibetan nun, was the spiritual teacher.

"I love Pema! I think I've read every one of her books. She is amazing. Have you read Eckhart Tolle?" she asked.

"I have seen him on YouTube but I haven't read his book yet. I hear it's pretty heavy."

They talked about spirituality all through the rest of the meal.

As they cleaned up the kitchen, he said "I have someone I want you to meet. I'll be right back. He is in the garage."

When he returned, he was holding a small squirrel in his hands. "Meet Fred, my pet squirrel, who I rescued last year. He had a broken back, but I nursed him and he can get around pretty good. He is a great swimmer, too."

"He swims?" she asked as she held little Fred in her hands. He looked up at her and seemed to smile.

"Yes, I take him kayaking. He loves going in the water. And he is a great chick magnet, I take him to parties. He just goes in my pocket."

"He *is* a chick magnet. Yes, I can see that. Your cuteness is now off the radar, Alex Kress."

"I know, I know, eh. I'm pulling out every trick in the book to impress you."

Later on, over a hot sake and green tea ice cream, Sarah told him about her life and her family.

"You sure you want the whole story? We could be here for a while."

"Absolutely! Do not leave out anything. I want to know everything about you."

Sarah went on to tell Alex about her folks meeting at the famous Findhorn in Scotland, where they were both volunteering. Within a year Sarah was born in a birthing hut there.

"I tell you this because my parents were real hippies, I guess. They lived off the land mostly and had a biodynamic farm. They had only one child and they home-schooled me. My mom was a Waldorf school teacher by training, but once they moved onto my dad's family hobby farm when my grandpa died, she quit teaching. We were poor, I guess. I didn't really notice. What we lacked in monetary means, we made up for in experiences. When I was ten my grandmother, who lived with us, passed away and my parents decided to build a studio for me all made out of cob. You know, straw and mud? It was a labour-intensive project but one that my dad said was a good way to deal with our grief. I got to paint it any colour I wanted, and I chose purple because it was my grandmother's favourite colour. They were eccentric but super amazing people. I got a lot of attention, and I feel I'm the luckiest person in the world to have had such supportive and loving parents."

"You keep saying *were*. Have they passed on?"

"Yes, they died in Mexico on a holiday a year and half ago. When I turned twenty-one, they rented out their little hobby farm and decided to travel. I was living in Banff by then, waitressing during the day and singing in lounge bars in the evening. They had always dreamed of traveling the globe once I got to be an adult. They had been to Thailand, Australia, and South America, and they were on their last stop in Los Cabos, Mexico when they both drowned body surfing."

"Oh, Sarah, I'm so sorry."

"Thanks. The first year was really hard. But I'm doing better these days. I look back and see I had a pretty incredible childhood. Unconventional but incredible."

"Tell me more," Alex said.

"Alex, it's two in the morning. I think you've heard enough about me. Next date, I want to hear everything about you! Now how about the hot tub you promised!"

"Alex! Sarah!" Lena Bea said as she grabbed her son and embraced him. Sarah stuck out her hand, but Lena said, "We are a hugging family. Come here, young lady." She embraced Sarah and lingered in her hug, rubbing her back, and then holding her hand as she led her to the kitchen.

"Thank you for bringing dessert. It looks wonderful. Are those real nasturtiums on top?"

"Yes, I hope you like it. The orange specs are marigolds."

"Where on earth did you find these in the dead of winter?"

"I have my ways. Actually, when my parents passed away, I bought a little house in Bragg Creek with the money from the sale of their acreage, and I transported their greenhouse to the property. It's a way to remember them, I guess. They were remarkable gardeners. These came from my greenhouse."

"Well, I've never even heard about eating marigolds. This looks like a work of art!"

As they sat down for appetizers before dinner, Lena Bea asked Sarah, "Now, Alex tells me that you're just finishing up your residency at the Banff Centre."

"Yes, I was lucky enough to get a scholarship to go. It was not something I could have afforded. And it's amazing. I have to pinch myself all the time that I ever got to go there. It was a dream come true for me."

"Do you mind me asking where your scholarship came from? Just wondering, as our foundation gives out one scholarship to the Banff Centre every year."

"No, I don't mind. It is The Gallant Kitchen Foundation. Funny name, but they are incredible. They support children and young adults from all over the world from what I understand, to pursue their dreams of a music career."

"Well, what a coincidence! That is our foundation!"

Everyone laughed.

"What are the chances of that?" asked Jim.

"Oh, gosh, I didn't even know. I never put two and two together. Alex told me you had a foundation to help kids but I never… Well, I'm so happy to be able to thank you in person! Thank you!!"

"You're very welcome."

"Do you mind me asking where you came up with the name?"

"I know, everyone always asks us that! My maiden name is Gallant. My father was from the East Coast, PEI to be exact, and my mother was from Nova Scotia. When my parents met, they had East Coast music in common. He and my mother hosted kitchen parties even before they got married. When my father died, my mother continued them. My mother was a song writer, as you probably know from applying for the scholarship."

"Oh, my God. You're Margaret Gallant's daughter? Of course. It just hit me! She is my favourite songwriter of all time! I grew up listening to her songs on the radio. She is one of the reasons I became a performer! I cannot believe you're her daughter. Alex never told me."

"I never even thought about it," said Alex.

"Sandy, my daughter, helps me with the foundation. You would have met her when you did your interview."

"I do remember Sandy! She was so sweet! A real artist in her own right if I remember correctly."

"Yes, she is the artist in the family, and she is doing quite well. She should be here in a few minutes. You know, I do remember reading your application. Jim or I usually read them all and whittle them down, and then Sandy makes the final decision. It was very impressive! I remember you talked about your wonderful parents and how supportive they were. It brought me to tears to hear they died so young. The whole idea of the scholarship came about because my mother, who was so talented, had absolutely no support growing up from her parents. As she got older, she became a support for so many people to live out their dreams," Lena Bea said.

"Yes, BB and I wanted the foundation to be about sharing the songs she wrote with the world, and then to use the money from the songs to help people of all ages live out their dreams in the music industry," explained Jim.

Alex put in: "Yeah, Grandma's songs have been sung by artists all over Canada, the U.S.A. Europe, Australia, and even Japan."

"I still can't believe this. Margaret Gallant was your grandmother? This is the grandmother you told me about? The one who made the best pickles and sourdough bread in the world?"

"Yup, that's the one!"

Everyone laughed.

Sandy arrived in time for supper. She volunteered at a homeless shelter and had been serving Christmas Dinner, as she had been doing since she was sixteen. The tradition was to eat late on Christmas Eve at the penthouse so it was easier for Sandy when she got off her shift. Then on Christmas Day they headed to the chalet and did a family outing, usually either skating or skiing or just going for a hike.

It was late by the time they went to bed. They had their Christmas dinner, sang Christmas carols, and then played charades till midnight. Sarah couldn't remember laughing so much. When she finally fell into bed, her cheeks were sore from laughing. She spooned Alex, taking in the earthy smell of the patchouli he always bathed in, and slept like a baby.

Alex got up early the next morning and left Sarah sleeping. He went to the kitchen, where his parents were having their morning coffee, and sat down without even uttering a good morning.

Sarah had been awake in bed for over an hour going over and over the conversations they had the day before. The stories swirled over and over in her mind. The ones about his grandmother Margaret, the story of the harmonica, and how she died.

She wondered if somehow her parents were looking down on her and had helped orchestrate meeting Alex. She felt she somehow knew this family, all of them. Suddenly, a flashback of a transcript she had read when her parents died hit her like a ton of bricks.

Sarah, age five and half

"Why are you crying, Sarah?"

"My husband got sick and died, and now I might die."

"Why do you think you're going to die?"

"Cause, I hit my head. That is why I have a mark on my head."

She touched the side of her temple and rubbed her birthmark.

She heard Alex get out of bed, and then talking to his parents in the kitchen.

"What do you think if Sarah and I got married?"

She heard a burst of laughter.

"Of course," Jim said, "You have our blessing, Alex. I think you will be very happy together. We see how you look at each other, and we were just saying this morning that we have never seen you smile so much. When you know, you know!"

"We were just saying how the two of you remind us of us," Lena Bea said. "I wish your grandmother were here to meet her. They would have gotten along famously."

"I know, I can just picture them singing together. And she is a great cook, too. I mean out of this world great! Well, you tasted her cake. We will have you over soon. She makes everything taste amazing, and even the way she serves food is incredible, it always looks like a piece of art! And she paints. I mean she is so good that she could make a living just selling her art!"

"Wow! Sounds like she is one talented woman. But I thought you two met while rafting? Is she into the outdoors like you?" Jim asked.

"Well, she likes being outside, but no, she is not into skiing, or canoeing, or kayaking, or anything like that. But she does like hiking, but it is a slow process! She is usually stopping every minute or so to look at a flower, a bug, or some bark. I mean she sees stuff that most of us just walk by. Actually, it makes me much more mindful. It is like being back in Nova Scotia at the ashram. You know, stop and smell the roses kind of thing. She is very spiritual."

"Mom used to say that to me all the time. 'Lena Bea, slow down and smell the roses. You're so busy trying to get to your destination that you're forgetting to enjoy the ride!'" Lena Bea laughed. "I was so eager to accomplish my goals that I forgot to relax. I needed a few accidents to slow me down! Ha. Now I get what Mom meant. Life is about the journey, not the destination. It is really great Alex, that you're learning all this now and that you found someone who has the same spiritual outlook on life as you do."

"Kids these days. They're way smarter than we were at their age, eh?" said Jim.

"Yes, way ahead of us!" Lena Bea said as she looked at Jim.

"Well, Alex, you have a pretty special woman there. She will be a wonderful partner for you. I have no doubt. You seem like a match made in heaven."

"I agree, and I hope if you have kids one day, they will be talented and charming like the two of you," declared Jim.

"Well, we haven't talked about that yet, but if we do, I'm sure you will be the best grandparents."

Sarah felt it was her cue to walk into the kitchen.

"You're all just having too much fun out here, I had to see what I was missing," she said with a chuckle.

"Just wondering what your children will be like when they are born," Lena Bea said with a giggle.

Sarah looked at the three of them and just couldn't help it, she felt so much love that she went over to each one of them and gave them a long hug.

"I really like this family," she said out loud and walked back down the hall to the bedroom.

Alex was on his way over for supper. She had finished her residency at the Banff Centre, and this was the first time Alex would see her little house. She was nervous, but not so much that he would see that she lived in a tiny house filled with easels and art supplies and plants with old second-hand furniture; she was nervous because she felt she needed to tell him about the transcripts. It was time. She knew he had studied Buddhism so he knew about reincarnation, but studying it and seeing it for real were two different things. She had enough trouble accepting it herself, even though it was so blatantly obvious.

Sipping wine after supper, she finally got the nerve to bring it up.

"Alex, I need to tell you about something, and I want you to keep an open mind." She could feel her hands shaking.

"Bunny, what is it? What's wrong?"

"I need to show you something."

She got the boxes of transcripts from the shelf and set them on the coffee table. She explained how her parents had kept them and that she had found them in their closet when she was cleaning out their house after they died.

"Remember when we were playing charades and one was about the harmonica inscribed with a marriage proposal?"

"Yes. But what has that got to do with these transcripts?"

"Read this," she said as she handed him the transcript.

IF I COULD LIVE AGAIN

He picked up the sheet of paper that was yellowed with age.

Sarah, age five

> *"What are you making with that box?"*
>
> *"It's an instrument."*
>
> *"An instrument? How do you play it? It looks awfully small."*
>
> *With your mouth silly. Like this. See you blow on it. My husband gave it to me."*

"Alex when I first heard about the harmonica when we were playing charades, I could feel the hair on the back of my neck stand up and goosebumps all over my body. I could see the transcript in my head as clear as day. I believe I am a reincarnation of your grandmother Margaret."

"Really, Sarah? Don't you think that is stretching it a bit?"

"That is what I thought, too. But then you told me about your grandmother's farm, her pickles, the goats. It is all here, Alex; it is all here!"

She took more of the transcripts out and read them to him.

"I know it seems so unbelievable. I have tried to ignore it, but then I hear something else that you, or your mom, or Jim says, and it is like I know what you are all going to say next. And then I read the transcripts, and they matched up with all the things you've talked about. The boy by the fence, that is Jim. Rene getting small before he died. Your mom told me all about her papa, and how he deteriorated before their eyes, and weighed only sixty pounds when he died."

"I don't know about all this. I need to think about it. I think I'll go home."

"Are you angry?"

"I just... I just want to go home." And he got up and left.

The look on his face was not something Sarah had ever seen. It was a look of great disappointment. She began to cry.

"I should have never told him," She thought.

"Hello, Alex, I am coming into Canmore today, want to meet for lunch?"

It had been three weeks since he had walked out the door of her house. She was devastated that he hadn't called her since. At first, she thought he just needed a few days to let it register but the days turned into weeks. She hadn't slept since that day, and she was desperate to see him.

"Hi, you have reached Alex Kress, please leave a message at the end of the beep, and I'll get back to you as soon as I can."

Lena Bea answered the door of the chalet.

"Sarah, what a nice surprise. Come in."

"I'm sorry for intruding without calling, but I was wondering if I could talk to you."

"Of course. Come in. Jim and I were just sitting down to a few appetizers and a glass of wine. Would you like red or white, or I can make you a cup of tea?"

"White would be lovely. Thanks."

"Jim, look who popped in, our Sarah!"

"What a nice surprise!" Jim got up from his chair and gave Sarah a hug.

They sat in the living room, she in a large, expensive, brown leather chair made from a wine barrel, and the two of them on the matching couch, close together holding hands.

"Honey, you look tired, is everything all right?" asked Lena Bea.

"No not really. Alex is not answering my calls. I am afraid I told him something, and he is having a hard time with it. Did he say anything to you?"

"No," they said in unison.

"Do you mind if I get something out of my car? There is something I want to show you both. Perhaps you can help me make sense of it."

As she laid out the boxes on the coffee table, she picked up random transcripts and began to read them, without an explanation except to tell them where she found them and when.

After fifteen minutes, Lena Bea began to sob. Jim put his arm around her.

"Sarah, you can stop. You don't need to go on. I see it. It is mom. Her soul was reincarnated into you. It all makes sense now. The minute I met you, I had this feeling of familiarity. Just the things you say, even some of your mannerisms like the way you put your hand on your hip when you stand, the way you tilt your head when you are laughing. Jim knows, I even said it to him several times. Didn't I, Jim?"

"Yes, she did, and the more we got to know you, the more and more I saw it, too. It was uncanny."

Lena Bea went on to tell Sarah about her near-death-experience. She had never told anyone about it except Jim.

"I have read enough about NDE's and past lives to fill a book. I was in another realm Sarah; you don't need to convince me. It is astounding that you have so much material here. Good for your parents for writing it all down. In most cases I have read about, I don't think the evidence is as clear as what you have here. Personally, I have read of many cases of small children talking about a previous life."

Jim smiled at Sarah as he squeezed Lena Bea's hand.

"Sweetie, I believe you too. I knew Margaret as if she was my own mother. The transcripts fit like a glove. It is astonishing really. As a police officer I was trained to look at evidence, and I can tell these transcripts are authentic and that your story is a sound one."

Sarah began to cry, but they were tears of joy. For the first time since she first read the transcripts, she felt happy, truly happy. She realized how important it was to be validated. She was still Sarah, but Margaret's spirit was with her. And it was okay, it didn't change who she was in the least. She still had her hopes and dreams like she always had. None of that had changed. She was lucky really because she had an understanding about herself that most people would never have.

Jim and Lena Bea got up and gave her a hug as she stood at the door.

"Don't worry, we'll talk to Alex. Everything is going to work out."

BOOK FIVE

Sarah, age five and a half

"I don't like this kind of bread."

"Why, what's wrong with it?"

"I only like sourdough bread?"

"Sourdough? Where did you eat sourdough bread?"

"I used to make it. We all did."

"You made it? At a friend's house?"

"No, of course not. When I was a mommy, I made it. Even my children made it."

"Did your other mother with the red hair make it, too?"

"Yes, and my aunt, too. It is the best tasting. Way better than this bread by a mile."

ALEX
2015 February 14

"Mom, I have a favour to ask you. Can I come over?

"Sure. What is it?"

"I'll tell you when I get there."

Lena Bea took Alex to her bedroom and showed him the wooden jewelry box on her dresser that her papa had made her for her twelfth birthday. She opened it up and took out a key that had yellowed tape wrapped around it, with faint-coloured letters spelling *Storage Bin*.

"Here, this is what you need. Go. I'll call the storage place and let them know you're coming."

As Alex drove to Millarville, he remembered his grandmother's crazy stories that she told him over and over about how she fell in love with Rene and how he proposed. He could still picture the kitchen parties when it seemed half the town would come over, and there was singing, and dancing, and musicians jamming till the wee hours. If his mom wasn't around, his grandma would let him stay up till the last people left. Even to this day, when he ate a homemade dill pickle it brought him back to those midnight lunches she served before everyone headed home— the ham sandwiches on homemade white sourdough bread, garnished with homemade mustard and his grandma's amazing pickles. "There is still nothing like it on earth," he thought to himself.

Bill's Storage, *Proudly Serving Millarville for over 50 Years,* the sign said.

Alex took the boxes, cedar chest, furniture, and instruments out of the storage bin and put them into the back of his Chevy truck, and then drove home. When he got there, he loaded everything into his living room. He looked at the beautiful cedar chest and noticed on the bottom right-hand corner that *Rene Gallant 1946* was carved into the wood. "He must have made this just after my mother was born," he thought. Grandma Margaret had labeled every box, and on the cedar chest it had a sticker that said *Harmonica.* When he opened the chest, the first thing he saw was a braid of red hair. He took it out and stood up, holding it against his body. It was taller than his six-foot-three-inch frame. He felt a wave of sadness. Surely there was a story behind the braid. He would ask his mom. He knelt down and there lay a perfectly folded off-white wedding dress, and beside it, a size small tweed suit that he guessed must have belonged to Rene. He gently lifted out the yellowed marriage certificate and some pressed flowers that were resting on the outfits, and he placed them on the table. The harmonica was under the papers.

He took the harmonica out of its case, and he read the inscription *Will you marry me?*

"You have been waiting for me, haven't you?" he asked the harmonica.

He put it in his pocket, went to the fridge, took out his mother's sourdough starter, and drove immediately to Sarah's place.

When she opened the door, he knelt on one knee and held out a jar in one hand and the harmonica case in the other.

Before she could even open her mouth, he said, "Sarah I have something for you. My mother's sourdough starter that has been handed down through generations, all the way from Ireland and maybe beyond, I don't know for sure. And a harmonica."

Sarah smiled. The box of transcripts that she found in her parents' closet was open on her kitchen table. Her mind flashed back to the page she had just read a few minutes ago.

Without a word, she took the harmonica and opened the case.

She read the inscription and smiled.

"Gimmie my jar!" she said, and laughed out loud. "Took you long enough!"

Alex held her face in his hands. "God, I love you!"

"Yeah, I love you, too."

Sarah, age six

"That is a beautiful picture, Sarah, who is it?"

"That is when I got married. That's me and my husband. and that is my auntie."

"It looks like you're holding flowers in one hand, but what is in your other hand?"

"It's a harmonica. My husband gave it to me."

"What is your auntie holding?"

"She gave me a jar with something special in it. But I don't remember. It was for my wedding gift."

The Ending...

August 2018

Sarah stood on the side of the main stage and listened for her cue from the MC. "Canmore Folk Festival welcomes our very own Juno winner and Grammy nominee, Sarah Kress!"

She flicked her bangs, a habit she had developed to hide her birthmark on her left temple. As she walked on stage, she thought about how great it was to be back from her U.S.A. and Canadian festival tour and in her hometown. She eyed Alex and their three-year-old daughter Jenny in the audience, jumping up and down and clapping and whistling. She could hear Jenny yelling, "That's my mommy, that's my mommy!" She waved at them and smiled. It hadn't been an easy journey getting to where she was now. Fame had its downfalls. Trying to juggle family as a touring musician created strain on all of them. But the second she stepped foot on stage, she felt whole. It was where she belonged. They would figure it out. Her and Alex. They always did.

She sat on the stool with her guitar, placed the harmonica holder over her head, and began to perform her Juno winning song "If I could Fly."

CPSIA information can be obtained
at www.ICGtesting.com
Printed in the USA
BVHW031342181021
618930BV00006B/102